GREAPA

Other Books by the Author

The Coming End of the Age

Preparing for the Lord's Return

The Goal and Peak of Our Christian Experience
Insights into Revelation, Book 1

The Beast, His Image, and His Mark
Insights into Revelation, Book 2

Firstfruits and Harvest
Insights into Revelation, Book 3

A Place Prepared
Insights into Revelation, Book 4

Delusion and God's Salvation

Visit aplaceinthewilderness.com for more about these books, including their introduction, table of contents, and ordering information.

Paul Cozza

GREAPA

RESOURCE *Publications* · Eugene, Oregon

GREAPA

Resource Publications
An Imprint of Wipf and Stock Publishers
199 W. 8th Ave., Suite 3
Eugene, OR 97401

www.wipfandstock.com

PAPERBACK ISBN: 978-1-6667-5152-9
HARDCOVER ISBN: 978-1-6667-5153-6
EBOOK ISBN: 978-1-6667-5154-3

VERSION NUMBER 081822

CONTENTS

PREFACE

My name is Samuel—or more properly, Salvatore. Although that was the name given to me at birth, I am very rarely called that any longer. It is a name buried in my ancient past under centuries of experience and generations of offspring. There are a few who remember it. I most often hear it from the lips of my wife as she speaks to me in love. And then there are those near to me from among the Blessed, those who passed through the Time. They remember it. But to others it is unknown, and that is really of no consequence.

I have lived for many years, as have all those of that time. Not one of us has died. We have all been kept by the word of the King. I am a living testimony, as are we all, that the King's word is true and never fails.

During the years of my life I have been enriched by time—not simply in children and in the wisdom that comes with experience. Rather, I have been enriched mostly in love—love of the King and of his God, love of his dear brothers, love of man, and love of God's marvelous creation. And, even after all these centuries, this love still grows. There seems to be no end to its increase.

However, there has also been much reflection upon the Dark Time and the events of that former age. My wife and I frequently converse about it—especially now, as we draw near the very end. And I, or rather we, have a story to tell, as do all of us who were there. It is a tale of evil forces and dark happenings, of wars and unheard-of violence, of catastrophes and upheaval. But it is also a chronicle of goodness and kindness, of divine arrangement and purpose, and of beauty hidden beneath the many layers of evil that encompassed that Earth. It is a tale of the King, of his return in glory, and of his kingdom!

Some who read this saga may have difficulty believing. It might seem too alien, too fantastic, and so extremely different from our present condition. Some may consider this to be a concoction of an old and failing mind. But I speak truth. The many who passed through that time with me will attest to this truth. The lord of our town will attest to this truth. Even the King himself will attest to my words. And when the words I speak of the future come to pass, then you will know I have spoken truth.

I tell you this to prepare you. Prepare yourself to be amazed and shocked, for what I will describe has never come into the mind of those born in this age, in this world, in the light. Even more, prepare yourself to be warned. Though we are in the light now, the darkness is coming again, at least for a short time . . .

INTRODUCTION

The little girl came running into the room shouting, "Greapa, Greapa, Greapa!" The man looked up from the pages of notes on which he had been studiously working. As she ran toward him, Greapa mused upon her. She was five years old, had curly blonde hair that glistened in the light, and had the kind of smile that could melt even the hardest of hearts. How delightful, happy, and endearing she was. She was perhaps the happiest of all his offspring. Nothing could keep the joy within her from bubbling forth. She was overflowing with life. Her parents had certainly chosen the right name for her.

Generation by generation he saw his children becoming more joyful, more happy, more excellent. It seemed as if the increase of joy—which he, all his family, and indeed all those living on the Earth were experiencing—was boundless. How wonderful it was to be alive at this time. Indeed, as he looked back upon his early years, how amazing it was to be as he was.

"Yes, Risa," Greapa replied, "What is it? Why so excited?" As she ran towards him he hurriedly put his notes aside, recognizing what was about to happen. The child jumped up into his lap and snuggled against his breast. How he loved her! How he loved all his children—for in reality they all were his and Greama's. And there was something about these young ones that captured his heart, just as Risa did.

"Mama says it is your birthday in a few days!"

"So it is," the man said, "So it is . . . " The family little knew what this particular birthday had in store. He and Greama had been preparing this for quite some time. These wonderful days were drawing to a close and it was time to warn his family, his neighbors, his friends. He was sure that others of the Blessed would be doing the same.

"But Mama says this is a special birthday. Why?"

"Because, dear Risa, on this birthday I will be 1000 years old."

Risa leaned up and kissed him on the cheek. Giving a child's big hug, she said, "Happy birthday, Greapa! I am five. Will I grow to be 1000 too?"

"I believe you will, little one. I believe you will," Greapa replied. "Now go fetch your mother and Greama, if you can find her," he said, shooing her off. "We have preparations to make."

As Risa's mother, Sarah, and Greama entered, Greapa considered the interesting dichotomy they presented—Sarah was young, quick, vigorous, while Greama was old in years, deliberate, wise. Yet they all lived happily together. What an extraordinary household, but it had been this way since the beginning. Greama and he would open their house to one of the young couples, who would then live with them for a few years. The couple would have a child or two and then move on into their own house, making room for yet another pair of young ones to live with them. It was a wonderful arrangement: the young were helped with housing and stability, and the old enjoyed the sweetness of the young and the bonding of parents with children.

Greapa rose to give them both a hug. His embrace of Greama seemed too affectionate to the younger woman, and Sarah said sternly, "Act your age," though mirth showed in her eyes before she could finish her words.

"I am," Greapa said, "I am not yet 1000. And I feel like I am twenty-eight!"

Sarah considered them both and marveled. She was thirty-eight and had watched her elders growing older. Some had reached the end of their years and died. They were quite aged, many more than 600 years old when they passed on. And they all died in peace. But this was not the way with Greapa and Greama. They seemed eternally young and certainly acted it! They looked barely older than she was. They were trim, fit, full of energy.

Greama looked kindly upon her great-granddaughter—she was not sure how many generations separated them—but she loved her husband too much to deflect his affections. Besides, look how handsome he was! "I think I am one with my husband, dear Sarah," she interposed.

Looking at them both with playful scorn, she had to agree. What a beautiful and loving couple she had for her ancestors!

Greapa then spoke with the weight of his age, drawing Sarah's immediate and full attention. She did not often hear this tone from him. "Greama and I have kept from you all what we are doing, and I thank you for respecting our privacy in this matter. Now it is time to reveal what we have been working on. My thousandth birthday is in three weeks. You and Greama must gather *all* who can come. Send out the call not only to family, but also to friends and neighbors far and wide. Whoever can come, must come. And this will be not simply for a day of celebration, but for three or four days of serious conversation. Let each stay as long as he or she can. Greama has been busy procuring lodging from those in our town. There will be food in abundance. All is ready, and it is time. When all have arrived and eaten their fill, the town bell will sound and we will gather in Great Hall."

Sarah was both captivated and stunned. Usually Greapa was deliberate and slow, but now he was quick, precise, and commanding in the orders he gave.

"Go, Sarah, go!" he barked. Awakened from her shock, she fled to follow his instructions.

Greapa then addressed Greama, "Is everything ready?" Greama nodded. "Have you enlisted all the helpers you need? Can we record every word?"

Greama looked knowingly and with deep concern at her husband. "Yes, Samuel, all is as we need."

"Then let us hope and pray that our words help save all of them from what is coming. Now go assist Sarah and use your inimitable charm to gather our guests."

1

WHAT IS

The word of Greapa's convocation spread quickly to family, friends, and neighbors. His invitation was an open one: whoever could come, should come. His summons spread to the surrounding towns and cities as well. This was not simply an invitation to Greapa's birthday celebration; rather, it carried with it a sense of significance and weight—Greapa and Greama themselves had prepared something. Exactly what that was had not yet been revealed.

Guests were encouraged to come not simply for a couple of hours, but for a few days until the purpose of the convocation was completed. If they could only stay for a short while, that would be fine; if they could stay for a longer time, that would be better. Whether they arrived earlier or later was also not critical, so long as they came. This assembly was something new, something unique, something of great importance. As the gravity of this gathering began to move the people, previous plans were put aside and hearts were set toward Greapa and Greama.

Greama had already spent much time in preparation for this day. She had contacted nearby friends and relatives—in fact, the entire town—soliciting lodging for a few nights to house those coming from afar, and had been able to secure accommodations for more than two hundred. She never said why she was asking for this assistance, only that it might be needed in the near future. Food and drink had been volunteered in abundance—her people were generous of heart and gave freely. With her helpers, Greama had also prepared their meeting place.

On the day appointed, guests arrived by twos, threes, or in small groups. Each saluted and congratulated Greapa—the aged one— for his seemingly miraculous thousandth birthday. There was great joy at seeing ancestors and old friends, and for the hungry or thirsty there were meats, fish, vegetables, fruits, breads and other baked goods, along with drinks of various kinds copiously prepared. Yet, beneath this celebration the moment held a sense of seriousness and urgency.

As the guests arrived, those who needed lodging were assigned accommodations, and to each guest the word was given that a meeting would occur later that evening in Great Hall. At the ringing of the town bell they were to gather there. There was an air of mystery surrounding all these proceedings. What had Greapa planned?

As evening fell, the bell rang, signaling the guests to gather in Great Hall. This was a marvelous stone structure crafted by master architects and masons. Not only was it beautiful in appearance, but it was also superbly functional. It had various entryways and more than adequate facilities. Excellent ventilation was provided by cross-breezes gently moving throughout the hall. And, in the center, it was open to the sky. While this limited its use during heavy rains, in their climate those were uncommon—the ground was watered mostly by mist that arose overnight. It was a perfect meeting place for this particular area.

Upon entry, the gatherers found hundreds of chairs arranged in concentric circles. Each of the chairs was handcrafted from wood, and each of them was so designed as to beckon a passerby to be seated. They not only *looked* comfortable, they actually *were*—the assembly could sit in them for quite some time without feeling restless.

As people entered and began to be seated, they noticed that on the far side, near the center of the hall, Greapa was sitting and watching. There was a look of concern on his face that was puzzling to most of the gathering. Near him there was a small table holding papers and a glass of water.

Greapa observed the scores filing in. He knew them all by name. He even remembered most of their births. There were offspring, friends, neighbors, and visitors from surrounding areas. There were young, old, and children. He loved them all.

Joseph, the eldest of Greapa's offspring, sat down beside him to his right, as was proper. Greapa reflected upon his oldest son (at least that is how he viewed him). Joseph's wife had died some years earlier, but at his age, which was now 682 years, he felt his time to pass on was near. So he had remained single. Death was not feared among them—rather, they looked to a resurrection and the Judge's pronouncement on that day. For most, and perhaps all, they would be entering into life as he and Greama had.

Greapa watched as Great Hall, which could seat well over 400, slowly filled. Greama and Sarah had done their job well, he thought. The hall would be completely full. Some would even have to stand in the back. *Standing room only* came to his mind—he smiled as he remembered that ancient phrase. How ironic! As the attendees settled down and the low buzz of the crowd subsided, Greapa sat in peace. Greama had certainly aroused a lot of curiosity.

After a brief time Greapa rose slowly and stood—slowly not due to his age, but due to the weight of that moment. He gazed round about at the many dear ones there, then looked up to the open sky, extended one arm toward heaven, and shouted, "Praise the King!" The throng responded instantly with echoed shouts of praise.

Greapa waited for quiet once more. He looked about, then with a smile he lifted his head again, raised both arms to heaven, and roared with his greatest booming voice, "Praise our God!" His words clapped like thunder. As his voice resounded, the hall erupted in praise. How wonderful it was to be here, he thought, as he let the waves of joy wash over and embrace him. How deeply he and Greama appreciated what God had done in bringing them to this point.

Greapa again waited for the hall to calm, then gently beckoned everyone to sit. He saw that every seat was taken and there were many standing, surrounding the circles of chairs. The number who had come to hear what they had to say was more than he could have hoped for. He took a sip of water and began.

"How blessed we are to be here, and how wonderful it is to see you all," he said to smiles and nods. "I can see by the great number before me that Greama and Sarah have mastered the art of persuasion." He looked over to his wife, who was sitting in an area set aside for her and her helpers. "The reason Greama and I have gathered you all is that we have something of great importance to share with you. And this is not only for you, but for the many, whether family or not. In our family, how many are there now? Many millions! I lost count a long time ago. And so for this word to reach our ever-growing family and whomsoever else might desire to learn of what we will share, Greama and her helpers are writing down all that is said. Between what they write and the notes we have prepared"—he pointed to the papers on the table beside him—"we should be able to put all that is spoken here into a book. We will print many copies and disseminate them. We hope to have this completed within a year.

"Greama and I have spent much time in our preparation—more than two years. It took us that long to assemble and order everything. I will do my best to relate all of this to you, but if I overlook something, Greama will then speak what I have omitted. In addition, Greama will share those events and experiences, for which she is far more capable." As Greapa spoke he saw the inquiring looks on the faces around him, silently asking what he was talking about.

"It will take some time to recount all we have prepared—our story is long—so expect to stay for two or perhaps even three nights, if you can. I realize there are those who might have to leave to care for necessities, though perhaps some will be so mesmerized and stunned by what they hear that they will find themselves unable to go! But whether you stay or leave early, be at peace. As I have said, we will print all of this in a book so that the fullness of the truth we speak can reach everyone. This evening I will not speak too long, and we will continue tomorrow after our early meal.

"As you well know, this current era—this age we enjoy—extends back about 980 years. Of course, none of you were alive for its beginning. Of all here, only Greama and I lived prior to that. Over the years, here and there, we have spoken a bit about what happened in the previous age, but we have only done so rarely, and never in detail. It is not a pleasant thing to talk about such matters, for either the speaker or the listener. But now Greama and I feel strongly that it is the time for us to recount everything we experienced, saw, and became aware of as it happened. The lord of our town not only agrees with this decision, but has encouraged us strongly to do so. Much of what we will share may seem unbelievable to you; however, it is all true. And, as you will see, my words bring with them a very serious warning."

As Greapa spoke, the atmosphere in the gathering became more still and somber, especially as he mentioned the word "warning." Every eye was fixed upon him; no one uttered a word. At long last they would all know what had actually happened so long ago, for among all the humans walking on the Earth none knew of those times except the Blessed. Many of those at the gathering had asked previously about those events, but Greapa or Greama had put off answering until now.

Greapa took another sip of water and a deep breath. "Are we not blessed?" he began. As he spoke, he doubted that anyone there realized how greatly blessed they really were. None of them had ever seen or experienced the great darkness. There were numerous nods of assent as Greapa continued. "Look at the heavens. They are crystal clear. The sun is extraordinarily bright and the moon shines brilliantly in its fullness. The stars we see at night are so numerous as to be uncountable. The great band of our galaxy stretches across the sky. The air that surrounds us and which we breathe is clear and pure. When we behold the wonderful beauty that encompasses us, it is like looking through a diamond. Every one of our breaths is fresh, exhilarating, and uplifting. The smells of lush vegetation and fragrant flowers tantalize us. The atmosphere is rich and excellent for life.

"Consider the streams, rivers, lakes, and seas. We have waters in abundance; everywhere water is cascading and flowing. The whole Earth is like a great watered garden. All the fresh waters are drinkable—there is nothing toxic in them. They are pure, clear, and refreshing. The great seas are also clean and their waves gentle, without threat. Even the sea-storms are mild. And all of these waters are teeming with fish and other sea creatures, which provide us with an amazingly abundant source of food.

"The Earth itself is verdant everywhere. Flowers of all types and blossoms surround us, and the land brings forth fruit abundantly. It seems that wherever we look there is fruit for us. When we till the ground and sow seed, the Earth yields to us plenteously. When we prune the trees, the trees yield tenfold. We are simply overwhelmed by the richness about us. Not one of us goes hungry—there is plenty for all, and more.

"Our livestock all bear numerous young, and none are stillborn." At this last word quite a few in his audience looked at Greapa quizzically, so he elucidated: "Stillborn means to be born dead—that is, the offspring has no life at birth." The faces of many seemed even more quizzical after Greapa's explanation, as if to ask how that could be, but he continued, "Even the wild beasts are our friends. They help us when there is a need; they never hurt us or the many other creatures; they never damage our crops or our gardens.

"Wherever we look there is a profusion of life—and what about the variety! Even the types of birds swarming through the air number in the tens of thousands. Their designs, colors, and behaviors are enthralling. Delights are simply everywhere.

"Even the insects are our friends. They do not damage, bite, or sting. Each is in its place, supporting the Earth's ecology. And how about us, about man? We are all healthy—*every one!* Disease is unheard-of among us. Many of us may not even know what the word means. And, how many of us have ever broken a bone? Very few, and those who do are quickly mended by God's sons. And we are exceedingly fruitful—our families are great in number. Even our babies are strong. Are we not deeply satisfied? We are filled with goodness and warmth. We work together to tend and enrich the Earth.

"Consider the foods we eat—the fruits, vegetables, grains, nuts, fish, meats, and many others. They are so varied and abundant they are hard to enumerate. Consider all the delicacies we enjoy. And all our foods are delicious and healthy. There is nothing stinted or toxic. Everything is life-giving and plenteous. What a God we have! We have in abundance and lack nothing. In short, we and the whole world are at peace. Even as we work, our rest is profound. Do I not speak the truth? And this all relates only to the outward things in our environment.

"Now consider your own talents. Each of us has skills to use and impart to others. The young apprentice learns from the old a skill of his or her own choosing. The skilled worker produces excellent handiwork. The aged master teaches the young and continues to craft masterpieces.

"You, the workers in wood and metal—how fine is your furniture! You, the makers of musical instruments—what can rival the sounds your works make? And they are of so many types! You, those who work with cloth and thread—how comfortable and pleasant are your wares!"

Turning to an elderly man, Greapa addressed him directly. "Bartimeo, which one of us does not enjoy a masterful chair made by your hands or the hands of those you have taught? Your carving is loved by us all, and at 482 years of age your skill seems to grow even more, although we wonder how that is possible!" Looking about, Greapa could see everyone grinning with appreciation, though the chairmaker himself appeared humbled by this sudden burst of attention.

Turning to another he said, "Gianna, is there a single one here who is not warmed in a chill by an exquisite shawl or coat woven by you or your tradeswomen?" Again, the attendees nodded and smiled. "Your workmanship is known far and wide, and how about your wonderful singing as you work! All who enter your house are double-blessed. I could go on and on, mentioning each of you: Pietro—your stonework; Marta—your breads; Lora—your care in teaching the children; Tomi—your amazing fruit orchards! Has anyone of us not savored Tomi's apricots?" Greapa could see not a few mouths watering as he mentioned those delectable apricots.

"God has blessed us all in the work we do. None of our work is unfruitful, and everything is plentiful. There is not a one of us whose works are unneeded; everyone is employed. And through all of this, the needs of each of us are met. When a young couple needs furniture, they go to the woodworkers. Marvelously, furniture appears. When the woodworkers need wood, they go to the lumbermen. Then, wood appears. When the lumbermen need tools, they go to the toolmakers. Saws and planes appear! There is enough for every need and more. There is no need to hoard. And the more we give to others, the more we receive from God. His blessing is everywhere.

"Now consider our person-to-person and town-to-town relationships. How often are there problems between us? Our doors have no locks, yet no one steals. The women walk at night in complete safety. The children sleep with security. There is rarely any social problem that might threaten us, and if one should arise it is swiftly handled. Even disagreements are quickly and easily resolved. Whenever necessary we bring matters to our town's lord for judgment, and they are taken care of. He is always just and wise; the righteousness and wisdom of God are in him.

"How sweet our relationships are, and they become deeper, more intense, and more precious day by day. Think about this: we know everyone by name. How wonderful it is to know the name of everyone in this hall—not only of those who live nearby, but even of those visitors from afar." Greapa looked to one side at a couple seated a few rows back and said, "Greetings, Jarod and Sasha. Praise our King!" Immediately the two echoed his praise with broad smiles.

"We are close in heart to many, and over the years we learn to gently pluck the delicate strings of our mate's heart . . . " With this surprising and unscripted word from Greapa—for it was not in their notes—Greama looked up from her writing to find him looking at her in love. A tear welled up within her. Looking about she saw that his words had reached the heart-depth of many listening. When he spoke, he had a way of moving his listeners. He spoke truth in love from his heart. How she thanked God for him.

Greapa went on, "There is no violence, whether it be man against man or town against town. We do not even have any weapons. Our knives are for cutting food or carving wood. Our stones are for building houses and landscaping gardens. We are at peace. Nature is at peace. Peace is everywhere. It is so intense that it is almost tangible.

"What is more, in the spirit-realm ruling over our cities are the many sons of God—and they are so many! They heal, guide, and shepherd us all towards that final goal. While they brook no egregious deviation from the path they have set before us, they also shine with indescribably beautiful light—light that encourages, enheartens, enlivens, and emboldens. You all have seen the lord of our town. Though he appears only on occasion, he is always present. As exquisite as the universe around us is, it pales next to him and next to all the sons of God. To sit with him and listen to his speaking . . . his words flow like a river of life into the hearts of those who hear. What a wonderful lord our God has given us. In all things he cares for us and our welfare. His gentleness, kindness, concern, and love are too great to fathom.

"Yet, there is even more. As beautiful as the creation around us is, and as wonderful as our lives with each other are, and as glorious as the sons of God shine, there is the One—the King in Jerusalem. We all have seen him year-by-year when we present ourselves before him at the Passover. His glory is the glory of glories—there is no one like him. He shines so brightly that were it not for him sustaining and uplifting us, not a one of us could behold him. The shining of that glory illuminates us, enlightening our hearts and minds. It uncovers any hidden root of sin and continually heals us from our fallen nature that is still within us. His virtue is unspeakably pure; his brilliance unimaginably bright; his richness inconceivably full; his kindness unbearably touching. When we see him, behold him—who he is, how he is—we are brought back to the path. We are healed from any error. We see the way—the way to the ultimate glory ahead.

"His beauty is unrivaled; of all the sons of God, he is the chiefest. We cannot help but bow down and confess him, not because of some force upon us, but by the truth of who he is and of what he has done, by his person and his station. He is the Lord of lords and the King of kings. All authority in heaven and on Earth has been given to him.

"His words are like rivers of clear crystal, like pure and transparent gold flowing forth to us. They give us life and freedom. When he speaks, it is as if a river of God himself is coming forth to meet us, heal us, fill us, and encompass us.

"And his words are forever. They never pass away. I remember even now with tears of joy, thankfulness, appreciation, and love the words he spoke to us—the Blessed—the first time we met with him." Within himself Greapa repeated them, *Come, blessed of My Father, into the kingdom.* Greapa turned to Greama and said, "Do you remember?" Greama nodded with a mixed look—trepidation, relief, joy, and love—somehow shaping her face.

"And what of his name. *His name!* The name above all names—Jesus. It is like an ointment poured forth, bringing healing, rest, and love. It is a balm to the weary. It brings life, health, and joy to all of us. How often do we all utter that name!

"Recall what he has done. Nearly 3000 years ago he died for us all—not only for us, but for all men and even the whole creation. It is due to him and what he has accomplished that we are all here today. Is there a single one who rivals him? Bless him!" Greapa gazed at the faces around him, all filled with awe at the King as they acknowledged these truths with nodding heads.

Then Greapa asked with his powerful voice, "In all of this, what do we see? *What do we see?*" Two bold young men stood and declared almost in unison, "We see God!"

Greapa smiled broadly with inward satisfaction. "Yes! We see God—God through his creation, God by the peace on Earth, God in his many sons, and God in and as the King—Jesus." Greapa waited for his words to settle into the hearts around him. He glanced at Greama and said with a voice that was somewhat troubled, though that was barely noticeable, "But it was not always so . . . " He turned, nodded toward his eldest son, and sat.

Joseph stood and addressed the many before him, "We will gather here again at the ringing of the bell after the morning meal tomorrow. Please take the rest of this evening and the early morning to converse about these things. May they find a home in our hearts, that they might become a salvation to us in the future days." Joseph knew something of what was coming, for he frequently read the Great Book.

He continued, "Also, recall what we spoke to you earlier, upon your arrival. While today's time together was for all, this is not the case tomorrow and going forward. What will be spoken next is only for the ears of those old enough to bear it. We believe twelve and older is a good guideline, though younger ones who are very mature for their age may also attend." With that he dismissed the assembly.

2

WHAT WAS

Later that evening Greapa and Greama sat at home with Sarah, her husband Joshua, and two guests, Nathanael and Mira. The latter couple had arrived late in the afternoon from a nearby town. They all talked of the blessings Greapa had described in his speaking earlier that evening. They had never quite seen it the way it had been presented. They supposed that perhaps they had been taking for granted the wonderful provisions they enjoyed.

Seeing the look on Greapa's face, Greama said, "We must retire for the evening. We have a difficult day tomorrow and must prepare. We should get to bed early as well."

In their bedroom Greapa spoke to Greama. "You did well, very well. Your preparation was excellent. The turnout was wonderful. You could not have done better."

Greama watched her husband with concern. He was speaking to her, but his heart was elsewhere. Greapa continued, "On the way back from Great Hall, I noticed the many conversations. Hopefully, they were talking about the many blessings we enjoy." He looked down and sighed heavily.

Greama touched her husband's cheek. She could see the angst gripping him. She knew his heart.

Seeing her beckoning eyes, Greapa breathed out what he was feeling, "I do not know if I can speak the help they all so desperately need."

From behind them came a gentle and familiar voice. "Samuel . . . Carolyn . . . " They turned to see the one speaking. They knew his voice well. Over the years, the lord who ruled their town—and who cared so deeply for them—had become a close and dear friend. He had come to them many times. Yet he always seemed to appear behind them, as if they needed to turn to see him.

The lord spoke, "You both did very well. You have laid an excellent foundation for what you will share next. We are quite pleased with all you have done. Your care and love for family and friends fill your words and touch their hearts."

"Lord, I do not know . . . " said Greapa, trailing off.

The lord continued, "When you both speak, we will help. We will witness with your words. We will show. We will make real what you speak. Trust us. We are with you and care greatly. Be encouraged. Be strong. What you both are doing will help save a multitude."

Greama interjected, "Why is it that you do not speak these things?"

The lord answered, "Carolyn, though we are still human, we are not quite the same. God is within us. He is one with us and we with him. God has uplifted our humanity to the standard of his divinity. All these dear people need your speaking—the speaking of those who are the same as they, the speaking of those who have passed through that time of great darkness and horror.

"In addition, as the day of trial approaches, we will all be hidden. Our words will be more easily put aside or forgotten. You, however, will be present as both a reminder and an anchor to them."

Greapa spoke hesitantly, "But if you were present and in view at that time . . . "

"Samuel, you know we cannot do that. That is not God's way. That is not according to his nature. He gave man a free will, and he honors and respects man's will absolutely. He does not cajole, pressure, or force. He allows each person to choose, even if the choice will be a tragic and disastrous one. While choosing what is evil greatly grieves God's heart, he nevertheless allows it. That is the price of giving us such freedom. In that coming day, our presence in glory would too greatly influence mankind. Each person *must* be free to choose either God or the evil one.

"Samuel and Carolyn, you both have seen and experienced the darkness. You have seen the extent to which the evil one will go. You passed through the great time of trial. You will not be influenced by the coming darkness. You will see it for what it truly is. The words you speak now, coupled with your presence then during the evil one's last time, will become a salvation to very many.

"Be at peace; words will come; we will work."

Looking into their good hearts, and seeing their deep hunger, he slightly moved aside the veil that covered what he truly was, as he had done occasionally in the past, to grant them the briefest glimpse of the divine glory, and in that dazzling moment he was gone.

As they slowly returned from their state of amazement, Greapa looked at Greama—relieved, uplifted, and invigorated: "Let us go through again what we will speak tomorrow. I am still not sure of the best way to begin, and there is so much."

Greama scanned her notes and proposed starting with . . .

They arose early the next morning, as was their habit. They were refreshed, revitalized, and motivated. They communed with God and conversed about the coming day. It would not be an easy one.

The morning meal consisted of eggs, oats, cheese, and fruit. There was considerable discussion at the table of the blessings they enjoyed, but Greapa and Greama could see that the younger ones—those born after the dark time—did not fully appreciate these blessings. And how could they? They did not have the black background in which Greapa and Greama had grown up.

The two older ones (actually, they were ancient by now) excused themselves so they could go on ahead to Great Hall. On their way, Greapa asked his wife, "Are you prepared, Carolyn?"

"Yes, my love, as best I can be," she responded. "You?"

"I believe so," said Greapa. "So much depends upon our speaking these days."

"Be at peace. God, the Lord King, the sons, and I are all with you. Speak your heart with strength and assurance."

Greapa was moved by her encouraging words. They had been together for 979 years and yet she still surprised him. She could still touch his heart.

They walked in warm silence to Great Hall.

At Great Hall he found yet another surprise. Though they had left quite early to precede the others to their meeting, when they arrived the hall was more than half full, and the bell of announcement had not even rung yet. *They are hungry to know the truth,* mused Greapa.

He looked to the sky above. It was clear—no clouds whatsoever. It was warm and dry. The sons had tended to the weather for this time. He thought, *They take care of so much in actuality. How blessed we are.*

Once again he sat waiting in peace as the bell rang. He watched the entrants as they filed into the meeting area. Each was looking his way in anticipation. He caught the eye of many, all nodding to him in encouragement.

After a good while, people were still coming. The seats were full, yet more sought to hear Greapa's words; even the standing area was full. People stood outside at the windows wanting to hear what Greapa had to say. Thankfully the windows were tall and large, and there was still plenty of ventilation.

The hall was filled and the areas outside by the windows were crowded. Yet Greapa could hear people still arriving. They were standing outside and out of sight, but still listening. Evidently, many had come late in the day yesterday. And of those who attended yesterday evening, few if any had left. He thought to himself that he must speak loudly. He looked about at the faces. They were eager, sober, and attentive. When he felt it was the time to speak, he turned to Greama, who gave him a nearly imperceptible confirming nod. Greapa stood.

He did not shout. He did not stir at all. He waited until all was quiet, and then slowly turned about looking at all those there. His words today would be very serious.

He thanked God and the King, especially for bringing so many to this meeting. He thanked them for such exceptional blessings. He then continued turning about, perusing the crowd, even while within he was struggling to find the right words. Finally he began.

"Yesterday evening we saw how blessed we are. Since God created man, no human beings—no merely human beings—have been blessed like we are. Last night we enjoyed just a small taste of that great blessing. In everything and in all ways we are blessed. But as I said yesterday, this has not always been so.

"We live in light—physical light, psychological light, spiritual light. But before the King returned to Earth it was dark, *very* dark. There was darkness everywhere. Spiritually, God was hidden, the King was obscured, the angels were unseen. Many believed there was no God, no spiritual realm. Psychologically, there was deception upon deception upon deception. The Earth was filled with lies and chaos. It was seemingly impossible to find the truth. Physically, even the lights in the sky were different. The sun was much dimmer, being only about a seventh as bright as it is now; the moon was pale; the stars were obscured. Darkness was everywhere and in everything. You might ask, Why? How could this be? It was because God had—and still has—an enemy: Satan.

"Behind the scenes, invisibly, this evil one with his forces was working incessantly to deceive, usurp, and overthrow. His method of operation was to hide, to avoid the light, because in the light he was exposed for what he is: a deceiver.

"Eons ago Satan was one of the highest—if not *the* highest—of the angels. At that time he was called Lucifer. He was assigned the temporary rule of the Earth, until those for whom the Earth was created were ready to assume that responsibility. He was, in effect, a caretaker.

"At that time the universe was filled with light; there was no evil. Yet mysteriously, Lucifer rebelled against God, and thereby became Satan—*the adversary*—for that is what his name means. He sought to ascend to God's position on the throne of the universe. He usurped the position of man and those who were to become the sons of God by seducing and deceiving man to fall into sin and, by this, enslaving man.

"Through fallen man, Satan then created a system of things on the Earth, called *the world*. Satan used this world, this satanic system, as a kind of counterfeit of God, to keep man from God and to mislead the sons of God. It was truly an evil and dark system. He was trying to replace God to man, and in every way attempting to overthrow God. Satan has always striven to get man to act independently of God. This was the real fall, man being apart from God.

"You cannot imagine how dark it was back then."

At that moment, it seemed that the universe blinked in some odd way. It was as if time slowed. Greapa heard an audible, collective gasp from those in the hall. He turned about and saw dismay on every face. Turning to Greama he saw her pained expression. She bent her head, sighed, and then nodded to him. With that look, Greapa understood what had happened. The lord had said the sons would witness with his words, would make them real. They had done this by letting the attendees briefly taste that ancient world of which he spoke. It was as if they had all glimpsed the past through a portal of time. Greapa waited for the audience to recover, then continued.

"I will not describe in great detail what that world was like. You could not bear it; indeed, to consider the things of that time makes me ill. It was truly much worse than I can ever tell. It was a godless world. The sons were present as lights, but what they were becoming was veiled. The world itself was dark, and many in it loved that darkness, for in it they could hide their evil deeds. Those in the world who loved the light—the sons of God—were generally despised by the evil-doers. They were denigrated because of their testimony. Many of them were imprisoned or killed.

"The whole world could be described with one word—*confusion*. Confusion was everywhere. The world was full of violence. Nation was against nation; person was against person. Murder was prevalent: theft, rape, fraud, greed, and every other conceivable evil were commonplace. Malice we cannot imagine was practiced. Men abused women and women abused men. Parents and teachers abused children. Violence of all kinds could be found throughout the Earth—especially in the great cities, which were then so widespread."

Again, the hall "blinked." As Greapa scanned the attendees he saw astonishment on their faces. He recalled what his listeners must have just seen, and this grieved him intensely. He could not imagine how these "innocents" must feel.

Greapa continued, "It was a world filled with every kind of immorality and perversion. It was rife with fornication, adultery, and worse: men with men and women with women doing unspeakable things; men pretending to be women and women pretending to be men. Not only did they practice such evils, but they made a show of them and boasted in them. They were proud of their evil. They took pleasure in others who practiced the same things. They were sick in heart, mind, and body."

There was no "blink" at these words. It was not necessary. The looks of revulsion were everywhere.

He went on, "Degradation was rampant: prostitution, mind-altering drugs, gambling—every imaginable excess." Greapa saw many puzzled looks. He nodded his head and responded, "I will explain these terms shortly.

"It was a world gone mad. Because men chose not to have God in their knowledge, God gave them up to all manner of depravity.

"That world was replete with amusements and entertainments of many sorts. All of these led people yet further and further away from God. These all served to temporarily distract men from the emptiness of their hearts and the vanity of a godless life. There were various types of games, some of them exceedingly brutal: men against men or women against women or even men against women—all seeking some way to gain an advantage against their opponents. There were huge stadiums filled with tens of thousands of shouting and screaming people, some of them half-crazed from the intoxication of the game to which they were addicted. And all of this was to watch athletes accomplish essentially *nothing*. There were many personal entertainments of many kinds—some visual, some aural, some tactile, or a combination of these—all attempting to fill the godless void, yet never succeeding."

There was another "blink," and this time the faces in the hall showed sadness and grief.

Greapa continued, "Greed was rampant. People attempted to amass huge amounts of goods, lands, and what was called 'money.' Money was a piece of paper or metal that represented a certain amount of value. In order to obtain whatever was wanted, people would have to give a certain amount of money in exchange. Even when something was needed, without money it often was very hard to obtain. The more money one had, the more things one could obtain. The more money one had, the more influence and supposed power one had in that world. If you had a lot of money you were considered wealthy and generally highly esteemed. If you had only a little money, you were often looked down upon as being of some kind of lower class.

"Nearly everyone was lusting after money. Even though it had no real value, people were deceived into believing that it did. Because they *believed* it had value, it *did* have value in their minds and in their environments. Men controlled others using money. The whole system of money engendered greed.

"Many people would do just about anything for money, even sell themselves or their bodies. If one sold his or her body for sexual purposes it was called 'prostitution.' Some would risk a certain amount of money, which was called a 'bet.' They would bet on the as-yet unknown outcome of some future event, such as who the winner of a certain game would be. If the bettor guessed correctly, then he would win the amount of money he had risked in the bet. If he guessed incorrectly, then he would lose the money. This was called 'gambling.' I know it sounds absurd to us today, but the greed in people's hearts to obtain money seduced them into doing all manner of inane things. The gross immorality of man under the deceitful influence of the vile Satan had seemingly overrun the Earth."

Greapa saw strained looks about him, so he said, "Let us take a short time to relax a bit and absorb what has been spoken," and sat down. After a minute or so, people rose and started to speak one to another. Greapa overheard the amazed conversation: "Did you see? What was that? Was it really like that?"

Greama sat beside him, "For a couple of brief instances, Dear, I felt I was back there again. It was so long ago, I had forgotten the sensations of that time." Her face showed the stress from viewing those ancient days. Greapa replied, "Our town's lord is not called 'Faithful' without reason. Lord Faithful said the sons would witness, and they surely did." Greama responded, "I never imagined it would be in this way."

After a short while Greapa stood and encouraged his listeners to be seated with the words, "We have much to cover this morning." He paused until the commotion subsided, then began again.

"In the ancient world there were nations, but not like the nations on Earth today. What we enjoy now did not exist then. Righteousness was seldom seen. Rulers in many countries were despots—tyrannical men—slaughtering and torturing their own people to stay in power. In other countries there were what was called 'democracies'—the people voted to decide who would be in power. But even in those countries there were abuses of many kinds: fraudulent voting and deceptions about or by candidates, for example. It was difficult to know the truth. Many of the people were hate-filled, railing against leaders, despising all who were not like them or who believed something different from what they believed. They were vicious, willing to say anything to tear others down. Such was the terrible world of man-apart-from-God .

"Nations were pitted against each other. Some conquered their neighbors, absorbing them; they were intent upon conquering the whole Earth, but were held at bay by the divine hand.

"In the world into which Greama and I were born there were three major powers. To the far east there was a geographically large and immensely populated country called China. It was a communist country—that is, the government owned everything and supposedly provided everything. It was actually a dictatorship. Those elites who comprised that government enslaved their own people. They attempted to control every aspect of the lives of their populace. They never spoke the truth, but rather hid it from their people. They did not tolerate dissent, crushing all who opposed them. They were completely godless. The Chinese people considered their government to be their god. But there was unimaginable darkness there. Despite China's outward appearance, beneath the surface there was great evil. It conquered many surrounding peoples and sought to subjugate the whole Earth. As we will see, were it not for divine intervention it may well have succeeded.

"To the northeast there was another large and ruthless country called Russia. It also had a history of overrunning those countries that bordered it. It pretended to be a democracy but was actually also a dictatorship. Opponents of the ruler would suddenly be killed or disappear or end up in jail. In many ways it was like China, but was much less populous and not as influential.

"To the far west across the great sea was the United States of America. It was a true democracy, with a transfer of power according to the vote of the people occurring every four or eight years. It was generous in helping other nations. It sought democracy in all countries, and consequently was a target of, and opposed by, both China and Russia. Although it was a great country, there were many problems within it: serious immorality, greed, deceptions of various kinds. It was used by God to keep China and Russia in check. However, as that age gradually came to an end, its power waned. It was weakened and divided from within by the hatred, dissension, shortsightedness, and lust for power of the godless among its people.

"There were many other nations—more than 200, in fact. On this continent where we now live, a group of them banded together into what was called the European Union. However, it did not last long, as will be explained this evening.

"And then, of course, there was Israel. It was tiny, but very powerful. It was surrounded by Arab countries, some of which wanted to destroy it. Many Israelis were killed by Arabs, some of whom were enraged to the point of insanity by their loathing of Israel, even killing themselves in order to slaughter some Jews.

"Nations had vast arrays of weaponry: naval vessels, flying machines called 'airplanes,' large and heavy land attack and support vehicles, and on and on. There was seemingly no end to the development of weapons: weapons were devised to counter other weapons; faster and more maneuverable airplanes were produced to overcome other airplanes; heavier and more powerful assault vehicles were constantly being developed. There were even devices called 'rockets' to send men into the space above our atmosphere. The increase in weapon power, speed, efficiency, and numbers continued unabated until the end came.

"And there were great weapons, called 'nuclear bombs.' Many countries had them, and others sought to obtain them in order to destroy Israel. These bombs could destroy entire large cities at a time." There was a "blink" followed by the look of horror on every face before him. Greapa paused, took a drink of water from the glass on the table near him, and allowed his friends, neighbors, and visitors to recover from the shock of what they must have just witnessed.

"Threats were everywhere. Deception was everywhere. Confusion was everywhere. And it was not limited to the governments of the nations. The worship of God was complete chaos. There were organizations called 'religions'—some great, some small—each of which had their own way to purportedly worship God. Many of these denied the Son of God completely. Others denied him in part. Very few held to the truth.

"Even among the sons of God there was confusion. They argued and divided over their different opinions regarding certain verses in the Great Book. They argued and divided from each other over differing practices. Many among them sought leadership positions and preeminence, to lord it over others and to enjoy material gain at others' expense. Some said the Lord Jesus was God; others, who were pretending to be sons of God, said he was not. Now, we know he is God become a man—but then, there were many differing voices. The result was division after division. It was unclear how to worship.

"Many even denied the existence of God." The shocked look of his listeners ranged from disbelief to tearful sadness.

"At that time their science had expanded at an incredible pace, to the point that there was such an overabundance of information it was overwhelming. They proposed theory after theory about things of which they knew little or nothing. They devised theories to justify their denial of the creation by God so that they could deny his very existence. According to them, we—man—came about by what they called 'random chance.' Though this theory was clearly and obviously impossible, many subscribed to it anyway. The alternative—that the Almighty exists and created all things—was simply unacceptable to them. Although there is no such thing as random chance, many readily accepted it as existing anyway. They were deceived by the evil one who was behind the scenes, in darkness, propounding foolish yet enticing ideas.

"Yet their science and technology, under the hidden direction of the evil one, produced a vast array of devices. Most of these ran by power similar to the rays of the sun, something called 'electricity.' All of these devices were designed to replace God, to lead people further and further away from God. Eventually, they even developed a minuscule device that they implanted in the human brain. It allowed communication from one mind to another, even at great distances. But subtly and evilly it allowed what was called an 'artificial intelligence,' which resided in a different device called a 'computer,' to control the thoughts, perceptions, senses, and feelings of the people who had received that implanted apparatus.

The artificial intelligence was so powerful, it could even create an artificial and imaginary world within the minds of these people."

The world blinked, and Greapa saw wide-eyed amazement; it quickly blinked again, and that amazement turned to horror. Greapa surveyed his audience. It was late morning and the people looked worn. He turned to Greama, who nodded. He decided to finish up his morning speaking.

"Given such chaos, consider the inward condition of man. It is difficult to imagine the inward confusion, chaos, hunger, pain, bewilderment, despair, and depression among men and women at that time."

More than one face looked to be on the verge of tears.

"People were inwardly lost, without hope, and seemingly having nowhere to turn. Men took their own lives. Others resorted to debauchery—strong drink and drugs of various sorts, all to hide from their true inward condition. But in the midst of such chaos, many of the sons enjoyed peace, security, and joy. The rest of us struggled, as if we were trying to keep from drowning in a sea of despair.

"It was a dark, evil, and seemingly hopeless Earth on which we lived."

Greapa paused, considered, turned to Greama, nodded, and sat down.

Greama stood, and the eyes of the crowd turned to her. "Greapa speaks the truth. Of all these things I also was a witness." She sat. Then, unexpectedly, from the back of the hall a pair of voices sounded, "We also were there. We also saw all these things. What Greapa says is true." Heads turned to see who spoke. Greapa instantly recognized Benyamin and Elizabeth, two very old and very dear friends. *They must have stolen into the back without being noticed*, Greapa mused. He much appreciated their presence and voices; his heart was warmed and uplifted. How wonderful to see them.

After they sat, Joseph dismissed the gathering with an exhortation to consider and discuss what was spoken that morning: "May these matters sink into our hearts and find good ground within us. These may be some of the most important words we will ever hear for our future."

3

THE BEGINNING OF THE END

Following their afternoon dinner, Greapa and Greama went back to their room to discuss the day's proceedings. Greapa considered, "It is hard to tell how much of what was spoken reached our friends—how many heard what was spoken."

Greama responded, "To me, Samuel, your words were like being there again. It must be extremely hard on all those listening to be subjected to all of this at one time."

"I wonder if there is anything we can do to help them," responded Greapa.

Once again that warm, welcome voice announced the town-lord's physical presence behind them. "Dear ones, you both must speak what you witnessed in those days—what you heard, what happened. You both should simply speak the truth. We will do the rest. However, all must be free to choose for themselves. Because of that, we can only do so much.

"Even though they have heard your words and will read them in the future, and even though they have been shown the truth of those words, some are having a most difficult time accepting this truth. Some disbelieve, and there are many more who will also follow in that path of disbelief.

"Disbelief closes off the heart to the words that would save. An open and accepting heart receives words even as shocking as what you have spoken. The good heart considers what has been spoken and seen, and muses on those matters. This then, in turn, bears the fruit of belief and assurance, both of which will become salvation to the open-hearted ones when the end comes.

"But to the closed heart we can only do so much. Sadly, very sadly, many of these will perish, though it is not God's will that they would. He grieves greatly over every lost soul, but—*but*—each must be free to choose, and the price of such freedom is having to allow some to choose destruction.

"As we did this morning, we will do again this evening and for all the remaining gatherings. These are terrible things we are conveying, but necessary.

"You have both prepared well. Now simply speak the truth."

They nodded. Greama then spoke. "It is hard for us to imagine what all of them must be experiencing within, having never encountered such darkness."

"For them it is nearly impossible to accept that such unimaginable evils ever existed," responded Lord Faithful. "But even now, your words are working within. Many questions they have had over these decades, and even centuries, are being answered. The many pieces of the puzzle of the past are falling into place, and they begin to see the truth. A great and healthy soberness and concern for the future is developing in many. For this we are greatly pleased and thankful."

Greapa then said, "Is there something more we can do?"

The lord replied, "What do you feel? Is there something more?"

Greapa thought briefly, considered, and said, "Perhaps . . . " He looked at the lord inquiringly.

The lord's eyes searched him. He smiled, nodded a yes, then vanished.

Greama peered at Greapa quizzically, who smiled back at her somewhat enigmatically and said, "Let us get back to work."

As they joined Joshua, Sarah, Nathanael, and Mira at the dinner table, Greapa and Greama noticed two extra, empty chairs. Before Joshua could reply to Greapa's questioning gaze, a heavy knock resounded at the door. Joshua smiled at his elderly relatives and motioned with his head to them, indicating they should answer the door.

Behind the door stood the broad-shouldered and beaming Benyamin with his petite wife Elizabeth—at least petite next to big Ben. Greapa smiled his greatest grin, laughed, and with tear-filled eyes bear-hugged Benyamin, who returned his joy in kind. Turning to Elizabeth, Greapa hugged her with some care, not wanting to pain the somewhat more fragile friend, and also not wanting to give any appearance of overstepping. Greama was no less affectionate with their dear old friends.

From behind them Joshua remarked, "Well, let them in! Seat them! Let us eat."

As they repasted on a typically delectable meal, Benyamin explained, "When we received word of your convocation, we immediately determined to come. Indeed, nothing short of our town's lord commanding us to remain at home could have prevented us. But on the contrary, he visited us and said he was very pleased that we planned to attend. He spoke what at the time seemed mysterious, saying in great seriousness, 'We will be with you. Bring your memories.' Then he left. I did not understand to what he referred, but upon hearing your speaking last night and this morning, I start to." Seeing Greapa's quizzical stare, Benyamin continued, "Yes, we were here last night, but we arrived somewhat late and so had to stand outside by one of the windows. We came quite early to Great Hall this morning, but found it nearly full."

Greapa appeared thoughtful, then turned to Joshua. "Joshua, quickly get a message to Joseph. Tell him to keep two seats beside me open for Benyamin and Elizabeth." Joshua immediately rose from the table and left to tend to the command. Greapa saw the food still on Joshua's plate and remarked, "A good—a very good—man is Joshua! His meal will wait for him."

Greapa and Greama both turned to their dear friends. Before Greapa could speak, Greama did. "Will you help?" Greapa waited hopefully. As Elizabeth nodded her assent, Benyamin said, "Evidently, it is for this that we have come. Yes, we will help and speak in whatever way we can. Given the solemnity of this time, we *must* speak, corroborate, and bear witness. Simply let us know when."

Greapa responded with relief and strength in his voice, "I cannot tell you how much your presence and your words mean to us—mean to *me*. Be prepared. You will be used."

As they finished their meal, Joshua reentered and, with a slight dip of the head, let Greapa know his task was accomplished. He then set to finishing his meal.

Before leaving for Great Hall, Greapa spent some time relaying to his friends how they planned to proceed that evening. He let them know at what points he believed their speaking would be most helpful. Benyamin and Elizabeth understood and agreed.

As the four walked to the evening gathering, the warmth among them was palpable, even though there were no words. Over the centuries they had become as close as human friends could be, and though they had not seen each other in some time, the love they had toward one another was undiminished.

As they approached Great Hall, they saw crowds at the windows with yet more people streaming down the various pathways leading to their meeting. Upon entering they found the hall completely filled, save for three empty seats next to Joseph and a sole empty seat for Greama beside those who were recording the words being spoken.

After being seated, Greapa watched and waited. The hand of his friend, who was seated beside him, rested upon his shoulder. He felt as if strength—*energy*—was flowing from Benyamin to him through that touch, and wondered whether Ben had learned some new "tricks" in his old age!

Once again Greapa stood. All eyes were upon him. He thanked God and the King for gathering them. He felt the encouragement from so many around him, and could see their hunger to know, to learn the truth. He began: "The words spoken this morning are true. But realize that it was really much worse than what I spoke. I do not have the words or the capability to convey the extraordinary wickedness present in those days. But we will continue to relate as best we can what happened to end that evil world.

"Tonight others will join the speaking—Greama of course, and Benyamin and Elizabeth, both of whom most of you know." Greapa looked to his friends. "Each of us was there; each of us will testify.

"Let me start by telling you a bit of my history. I was born and raised not far from where we now are, in the country then called Italy. My father owned a vineyard, and I grew up learning the ways of the vintner. Where we lived was not especially populated. We enjoyed living in that small community, but surrounding us was much evil. And although we were small, we were not impervious to it.

"In those days man had devised a means to transmit pictures—moving pictures—from one place to another almost instantaneously. It was called 'television.' Through that we, or anyone else, could see what was happening in other places, even very remote areas. Television was filled with all manner of evil—some of which was actually happening, while some was simply dark fiction.

"Even though I lived in a rural community, through television I could see what was happening in other parts of the world. And as the end came, so did the evil—even to our little community."

Greapa looked to Greama, then sat. At his cue, Greama stood to tell something of her past. "I was born on the great continent across the sea to our west, in the country called the United States. I was raised in one of the fairly large cities of our time called Boston. My mother was a nurse, caring for the sick and injured. My father was an executive—an administrator—of a large construction company that built edifices of all kinds, large and small, above ground or under ground." Once again, bewildered expressions appeared on the faces of those listening. This led Greama to explain: "A company was a large organization of people who manufactured certain products or provided certain services. The buildings during that time could be quite enormous, even over 800 meters in height, so there was a need for large, coordinated groups of people—companies—to carry out such huge undertakings." This short explanation did not seem to allay the puzzlement, but Greama continued her story.

"As an executive, my father traveled all over the world, to China, to Europe—the continent we are now on—and to many other places. As I grew, I would sometimes accompany my father in his travels. I saw firsthand many of the matters of the endtime." She turned toward Benyamin, then sat.

Benyamin stood. He was large, imposing. As he spoke his voice was deep, like the sound of the town's great bell. His words carried the weight of his many years. "I was born to the east in a country called Turkey, midway between here and the beautiful Israel. I grew up on a large apricot orchard owned by my uncle—my father's brother. When I was very young my father, who was a critic of those in power in that country, was taken away by the security forces of that government. He never returned. Although we never found out what happened to him, we believe he was tortured and murdered by those security personnel. When he was taken, my uncle quickly took us from our home and hid us on his orchard until he felt it was safe for us to be seen again. I too was an eyewitness to the evils of that time."

As he sat, Elizabeth rose beside him. Although she was relatively small, her voice was strong and clear. "I was born and raised on the large island off the western coast of this continent on which we now live. In those days the island was called Great Britain. I grew up in the part of it called England. We lived in the countryside, away from urban areas, and we were quite poor. My father and mother did all manner of work to feed our family. I was the oldest of four children. When I was very young I also started working to support the family. I saw much of the evil of those days, and some of the good. It pains me—it pains us all—to recall these matters, but it is necessary for you that we do."

As she finished, Greapa rose and spoke again. "That world had become crazed. Although I was young, I still could perceive the growing insanity—people speaking and doing bizarre and inane things; people attacking others both verbally and physically; people willing to do anything, absolutely anything, to silence anyone or anything with which they did not agree. All semblance of normality, of rationality, was discarded by many. And, when it seemed this situation could not possibly get worse, it became just that—much worse.

"The sons of God, who were called Christians at that time, received the worst of this abuse. Because the evil one hated God, he hated God's sons. Because he hated them, so did his evil followers. The Christians were maligned, despised, and persecuted. As the end drew near, many were tortured and killed. This was particularly so in China, Russia, and even on this continent.

"Israel was also greatly loathed. Many sought to eradicate it, but sovereignly God would not allow this. Although this worldwide situation was terrible, even more horrifying times were about to come upon the Christians, the Jews, and the whole Earth."

Greapa took a sip of water from the glass on the small table before him, considered for a few moments, then resumed speaking. "Here in the country of Italy a very strong government was attempting to impose strict laws and regulations on the people. As I mentioned this morning, the European Union had fallen apart. Its bureaucracy—the elite who governed the people—became overbearing in their demands upon member countries. They sought to regulate according to their opinions how countries were run, what laws countries enacted, how criminal and civil courts judged. Upon those countries that did not submit to their rule, they levied fines and other burdensome penalties. Eventually, first one, then others left the Union, having had their fill of such arrogance and oppressive overlording. The European Union then collapsed."

Greapa turned to Elizabeth, who stood and spoke. "The country in which I lived was the first to break away from that overbearing union." The segue from Greapa to Elizabeth was remarkably smooth and seamless, as if they had practiced it many times. "I recall that we called it Brexit—the British exit from the European Union. This was followed not long after by countries in the eastern part of the union, Italy, and other countries around the Mediterranean departing."

Greama then stood and continued the narrative. "The United States was a great country that held at bay the world's most evil powers, including China and Russia. But it was being torn apart from within by godless people and evil forces. Satan was determined to neutralize the United States by paralyzing it and ultimately destroying it. He wanted to unleash China and Russia upon the Earth, and in so doing crush and obliterate everything of God. There were very many at that time in the United States who stood against God, against morality, against whatever was good. They demanded and promoted the slaughter of the unborn, the confusion of the sexes, and the overthrow of lawfulness. Many were violent, vitriolic criminals with bloody hands and hearts, who in nearly every way were one with Satan. They levied slanderous charges against those who opposed them, accusing them of all those things of which they themselves were guilty: bias and discrimination due to race or gender, great intolerance of opposing views, hatred, violence, and the like. Then, using subtle and evil means, they inserted their champions into power.

"No good came from this. The country became enfeebled and unable to stay the tide of evil that was swelling in China. China was on the eastern side of the large continent called Asia. It bordered the largest ocean on Earth called the Pacific. Taking advantage of such a situation in the United States, which it had had a hand in causing, China invaded the island countries in the Pacific. With world domination within its reach—something for which it had long lusted—China chose to use military force to overthrow the governments on those islands and seize power. It swept over all the oceanic islands, large and small, that were near it. It even went so far as to invade the large southern continent called Australia, although its armies were stopped there by Australia's forces with the help of its allies."

Greama sat down and Benyamin stood to continue the narrative. "Israel had been making peace with many of its Arab neighbors. However, a few nearby countries still sought its destruction. There even were many living within Israel itself who sought to destroy it and kill as many Jews as possible. Where I lived, the sentiments were mixed: some hated Israel, others could not understand such hatred and did not agree with it. I was one of the latter."

Greapa summarized: "So this was the situation as the end approached. The European Union had collapsed. From the remains of its demise a new confederacy was forming. The US was weakened, paralyzed, and hobbled by internal evil forces. China was expanding throughout Southeast Asia, the Pacific islands, and Northern Australia. Israel was making peace with many Arab countries, while others still were attempting to destroy it. And behind the scenes Russia was meddling almost everywhere.

"From the ashes of the European Union there rose up a confederacy of ten nations, most of which resided along the Mediterranean coast. Italy was one of those ten. That kingdom—for that is what it was in actuality—was quite strong with very powerful leaders, although their strength was tempered by the conflicting voices of their people.

"I watched as this alliance formed. As its security forces demanded greater and greater subservience from the people, my father became an active opposer of this new union. One day as he was protesting in the streets of a nearby city, he was killed by those very forces that were supposed to provide security. Although I was only 11, I determined from that moment never to give my allegiance to that confederacy.

"The sovereigns of those ten nations, reveling in their power, considered themselves kings and behaved as such. But in the midst of them a largely unknown and barely regarded person started to assert himself. Unbeknownst to his competitors, he had secured sole access to certain devices of unimaginable power. Those devices allowed him to outwit, outplan, and outmaneuver anyone who resisted him. More importantly, unseen to all, Satan was enabling and empowering *him*.

"As he ascended to power, three of the ten kings opposed him, but using those devices he overthrew them and installed others who were sympathetic to his ambitions. Those devices combined with Satanic supernatural support seemed to make him invincible. He soon declared the confederacy to be an empire—*his* empire—and himself to be emperor. Indeed, it seemed no one could stand against him. He considered himself to be the greatest human who ever lived. He was tall, handsome, forceful, and spoke with incomparable charm. Many—*many*—were taken in by his polished and deceptive manner.

"Then the persecution of God's sons started in earnest. We began hearing reports of Christians being slaughtered in parts of the new confederacy, in Russia, and particularly in China and on the islands it had conquered. We saw pictures on television—pictures smuggled out of China—of summary executions of Christians." A blink, then the faces about Greapa turned solemn and grieved. *How hard it must be for all these to witness such things*, he thought. Nevertheless he continued, "They were killed solely because of their faith in God and Christ. I admired their great courage as they stood before their executioners undaunted, and died with glowing faces filled with anticipation of what awaited them after death.

"This persecution started slowly, but grew day by day. How many thousands—how many millions—were murdered, only God knows. China did all it could to hide its massacre of those who loved Christ, but it could not be concealed. As China began its subjugation of the Pacific and started martyring Christians, many people on those as-yet-unconquered Pacific islands fled to the United States, flying in airplanes across the ocean. Others from the confederacy and elsewhere also fled, as the persecution was becoming rampant and nearly universal. Even though parts of United States would not receive them, thankfully they were welcomed in its God-loving center and south. The United States, or at least part of it, became a haven for persecuted Christians."

Realizing that they had been speaking for some time, and that their rapt audience likely needed to rest for a bit, Greapa then said, "Let us stop here for a short time, then reconvene." The listeners moved about, speaking to each other in amazement about what they were hearing. A few took out some fruit or other morsels, which they brought with them for added nourishment should they have a short interlude such as this.

The four who had been speaking huddled together. They discussed when to end their speaking for the night. It was not easy for their listeners to absorb so much of what was completely alien to their experience, so they did not want to speak for too long a time in any particular meeting.

Greapa stood, and when all present were seated and quiet he resumed. "Then something earth-shattering happened, something that caused enormous upheaval and tumult in every part of the globe, something that drastically changed the course of human history." As he looked about at the faces filled with anticipation, he surmised that his audience expected him to say that it was at that point the King returned. *Sadly, the situation on Earth was about to become much worse,* he thought. "At that time, on the mount where the Temple now stands, there was a structure called the Al Aqsa Mosque. It was revered by the adherents to a religion called Islam, which was one of the many Christless religions that distracted and led people away from God. That mosque on the Temple Mount was placed there for the sole purpose of keeping the Temple from being rebuilt. A previous Jewish temple had been destroyed thousands of years earlier and needed to be rebuilt for Christ to return to the Earth. In effect, that mosque was preventing the King's second coming.

"Furthermore, if anything remotely resembled an attempt to damage that mosque, the Muslims—the followers of Islam—would become enflamed in a religious fervor and would attempt by any means possible to protect the mosque, one of their numerous idols, from harm. But something astounding happened . . . "

As Greapa paused, Benyamin picked up the story. "A military airplane crashed into that mosque, completely obliterating it."

At this word the universe again blinked, but this time everyone, including Greapa, witnessed the event. It was as if they were hovering above the mosque and about 750 meters to its southeast. A military plane—a sleek jet designed for extreme speed and agility in battle—appeared, traveling at tremendous velocity. It smashed into the mosque, completely disintegrating both itself and the mosque. Debris was thrown in every direction, greatly damaging surrounding structures. From what they were seeing, it was obvious that this was no accident.

Stunned by what he saw, Benyamin nevertheless continued his description of events. "This appeared to have been done purposely. The Arabs blamed Israel and collectively threatened to invade and destroy it. There were riots in Arab cities everywhere, accompanied by vehement demands to overrun Israel and kill or expel all the Jews.

"Israel, in turn, blamed Arab terrorists—people who killed others for the sake of their cause, even killing themselves for the sake of mass murder. However, Israel's voice went unheeded even though it produced evidence to substantiate its claim. The religious zeal of the Muslims deafened their ears to the reasoned speaking of the Jewish leaders.

"Arab armies massed for an all-out attack on Israel. Faced with such a great existential threat, Israel declared what had long been presumed: it possessed nuclear weapons. Furthermore, Israel publicly announced that it would use those weapons against any and all nations that attacked it. Then Russia and China threatened to bomb Israel if it used nuclear weapons, and the United States and Great Britain, in turn, threatened to destroy Russia and China if they attacked Israel. The whole Earth was on a knife's edge.

"The Arab nations were justifiably cowed by Israel's warning that it would destroy them, but their populaces were in an uproar. The Arab leaders could not calm or control their own people. All the great militaries of the Earth were in the highest state of alert. It seemed there was no way to resolve this standoff."

Greama then spoke. "As this intense confrontation grew toward the point of explosion, the Christians around the Earth were ecstatic. The destruction of the mosque on the Temple Mount was a clear sign of their Lord's impending return. The hearts of many of the sons of God burned in anticipation of the coming of the One whom they so dearly loved. In the United States there was also a great upheaval, but not as it was elsewhere. Rather than riots and violence as were being seen across the globe, the Christians were rejoicing; many who had been living rather common lives became zealous for their Lord. There was a kind of great awakening. The good news of Christ, of what he had already accomplished, and of his return was proclaimed throughout that country. Many expected Jesus to return at any moment; others announced that his return was still some years off. But nearly all believed his coming was imminent.

"On corner after corner throughout the large cities and even in small towns, Christians stood and proclaimed Christ. Some announced the end of the world, while others spoke of Christ's second coming; still others spoke of the removal of the Christians from the Earth by what they called 'the rapture.' There were many different opinions regarding coming events, which led to much confusion. This greatly hampered their efforts to preach to the nonbelievers, many of whom dismissed their speaking because of the conflicting claims. Nevertheless, their speaking produced an enormous effect upon the atmosphere and the culture within the United States. Many rejected the amusements and enjoyments of that world. In addition, the severe global situation helped turn many people to God for solace and even the more for meaning."

Greama then stopped speaking and Greapa took over. "In the midst of this worldwide crisis, the leader—the self-declared emperor—of the Mediterranean empire stood up to calm the situation. He had become renowned for his problem-solving ability. Indeed, it seemed there was no problem he could not solve. Even the most intractable matters were but child's play to him. Few knew that he had both incredibly powerful devices *and* Satan himself helping him.

"He contacted leader after leader, government after government, country after country—first Israel, then the Arab countries, followed by Russia, China, the United States, and Great Britain—and, using his unequaled charm and brilliant mind, he persuaded these countries to give him time to find a solution to what at that moment seemed insoluble. The world took a step back from annihilation.

"The Arab countries were demanding that Israel give up its nuclear weapons. Israel refused, knowing these were its deterrent against threats from the Arabs. The Arabs were demanding to rebuild the Al Aqsa Mosque on the Temple Mount; Israel again refused, since the mosque was destroyed by an *Arab* terrorist and they disagreed strongly with rebuilding what, in their eyes, was a heathen structure on their most holy place on Earth. Furthermore, powerful factions in Israel's government wanted to rebuild the Temple on that spot. Israel demanded an end to incitement and terrorism, and wanted its control over Jerusalem to be recognized by all nations. The Arabs balked, wanting Jerusalem at least under joint control between Israel and them. Who could resolve these issues?

"That great emperor, to whom I will not refer by name since that name is accursed, appeared to find a way. It was a way filled with deception, but very few at that time understood that. His six-part solution was this:

1. Israel was to give up its nuclear weapons *and* stand down its military.

2. The emperor would guarantee Israel's security with his own military.

3. Israel could rebuild the Temple on the Temple Mount after clearing debris from the building site.

4. Arab countries would stand down their militaries, disarm, and cease all incitement against Israel.

5. This pact would last for a period of time, near the end of which it would be revisited to determine whether it could and would become permanent.

6. The terms of the pact would be overseen and secured by the emperor and his forces.

"No one realized that the emperor had foreseen this situation for some time, and had planned for it. In fact, he had his hand in the events that had occurred, and was using all this to entrench himself in Israel and the Arab countries, so that he might have a base from which he could further expand his empire to the east and south."

Benyamin then gave further details. "This grand compromise was difficult for everyone to swallow. Israel would have to give up, at least temporarily, a military that was renowned for its prowess in war and clandestine action. But in return it would get peace, or so it seemed. Furthermore, it could rebuild the Temple. This latter point influenced many Jews to accede to this pact.

"Although they would have to give up any claim to Jerusalem and the Temple Mount, the Arabs would eliminate Israel as a military threat. Secretly they planned to attack Israel, retake the Temple Mount, and destroy the newly rebuilt Temple once the emperor's protection was removed.

"There was much debate about the term of the agreement. Eventually, a period of approximately seven years was agreed to. It was to begin when the emperor's security forces and inspectors were in place within Israel and the Arab countries, and end about seven years later on the Jewish feast of Rosh Hashanah. In all, the pact would last somewhere between 2500 and 2550 days, depending upon when the emperor's personnel were in position.

"However, because of the divisive nature of the requirement that it give up its military, Israel would only agree to and ratify this accord by holding a referendum on it." Seeing puzzled looks about him, Benyamin explained the word "referendum," then went on, "As the referendum drew closer, both sides—those for and those against the pact—sought to persuade the public how to vote. As this great debate raged, a very persuasive and energetic speaker came to the fore in Israel. He led many to vote for the accord, saying it would both guarantee peace and allow the Temple to be rebuilt. I saw and heard him on television. He was indeed convincing, but there was something about him that did not seem right—something hidden, something deceptive, something dark.

"The referendum on the pact was approved by a huge majority, with about two-thirds of the people of Israel voting for it. This meant Israel was to give up its military, particularly its nuclear weapons. It passed largely due to the speaking and influence of that orator. Preparation started immediately. Security personnel from the empire were trained to secure the peace in Israel. Inspectors flew to Israel and the Arab countries to ensure that the provisions of the pact were being faithfully carried out."

Elizabeth joined the narrative. "In Great Britain and the United States, Christians were excited beyond measure. Many prophesied that the Lord Jesus would, at any time, take them all to be with him. Others were sober-minded, believing that much preparation—both within themselves and in their environment—was necessary before the King's return. Some spoke of great calamities coming upon the Earth. Many non-Christians scoffed at what they took as nonsensical babble. Although I was not a believer, something about the speaking of the Christians struck me as meaningful and important.

"Those who believed many Christians would remain on the Earth through the coming cataclysms began to prepare underground shelters and supplies of food and other necessities. They saw that whether they were taken or not, these shelters and supplies would be needed by those who did remain on Earth. They were joined by others who saw the logic and goodness of that reasoning. Soon an all-out effort was being made in preparation. Coupled with the care for the welfare of those persons fleeing persecution, this joined many willing-hearted Christians in one mind to prepare for Christ's return.

"The mockery from non-Christians was extraordinary and severe. While the Christians worked with one goal and warned of impending disaster, even announcing it in the printed media of that time, the nonbelievers excoriated them. Even in the face of such heavy denunciations, the believers simply continued their preparations."

Greapa saw the great interest and anticipation around him, but also realized it was getting late into the night. He said, "Let us stop here this evening and continue again tomorrow morning." There was some disappointment at that word, but the need for rest and sleep was acknowledged. The attendees stood and began talking excitedly. Hardly a one left Great Hall. Finally Greapa addressed them again, this time in a loud voice, "Please go home and rest. You will need all your strength tomorrow!" With that, the people began filing out.

Greapa turned to Joseph, "After the morning meeting tomorrow, come to my home immediately. I have a task for you." Joseph looked puzzled at the unexpected request, but nodded in agreement.

Greapa then spoke to Benyamin and Elizabeth. "Can you come for breakfast in the morning? I'm still not sure how to speak of the events in Israel during the last days. None of us were there, and so we are not able to present a fully accurate account. What we were shown at the time was mostly propaganda."

4

THE SNARE

At home that evening, Greapa and Greama enjoyed some time with Joshua, Sarah, and their guests. Coupled with an evening nosh, it was pleasant relaxation from the demands of the day. As the hour latened, they excused themselves and went to their bedroom.

As they opened the door, they saw Lord Faithful sitting on a chair in the corner. Before Greapa could speak, he said, "Do not be anxious. All matters have been taken care of. Be at peace. The answer to your concerns will arrive in the morning." He then vanished before Greapa or Greama could utter a word.

Greama then said, "Since everything is taken care of, it seems that we can simply go to sleep." A somewhat flummoxed Greapa agreed.

Over breakfast—a plate of fruit, cheese, and ground grain—Greapa and Greama were discussing with Ben and Elizabeth the curious visit from Lord Faithful the previous night. They were not sure what he meant by his words. As they spoke, a deliberate but gentle knock sounded at the door. Greapa asked Joshua, "Are you expecting anyone?" Joshua shook his head and rose to answer the knock.

Standing at the door was a man of medium build, somewhat dark skin, and wisdom-filled eyes. His features indicated he was of Mediterranean descent. Joshua would have guessed him to be a Jew, but the guess was moot because of the clothes he was wearing, for the vestments of the Jerusalem Levitical priests were unmistakable. It was an extreme honor to be visited by a citizen of Israel, but it was unprecedented for one of the priests to grace a home, for they stayed in Jerusalem by the King to serve him. The priest spoke quietly, "I seek Greapa."

Though stunned by what he saw, Joshua managed to extend a welcome, "Come in. Come in, sir. Please."

The priest entered the house and surveyed the interior. Seeing the diners at the breakfast table, he walked over to them and announced, "I seek Greapa."

Before Greapa could respond, Sarah was up and heading to the kitchen to provide breakfast for this most honorable visitor. Greapa stood and offered the priest his seat, while saying, "I am he. How can I be of service to you?"

The priest sat in Greapa's chair, although from his manner it appeared he would have been happy to sit anywhere. He began, "I am sent by the King." With this word all at the table sat straight and listened with utmost seriousness, eyes wide. "I am Moshe. I stand by and serve the King. He directed me this very morning, 'I am sending you to the house of one named Greapa. Seek him out, for he has urgent need of you.' He then spoke one more thing, which I did not understand, 'Bring your memories.' So then, how can I be of service to *you*?"

Sarah placed a plate of the choicest breakfast foods before their esteemed guest. He surveyed it with pleasure, wisely chose a perfectly ripened apricot, and began eating it between the sentences of his speaking.

Greapa was astonished. *The King had sent his trusted servant to them! This is what Lord Faithful meant when he said matters were taken care of.* He was overwhelmed by the care being shown to him. He found his wits and relayed to Moshe what had been happening the last few days, and what their need was.

The priest replied, "So that is why there is the need for my memories! I was there in Jerusalem throughout the whole time of those last years. I was an architect during that time, and I helped *build* the Temple! I can address all the matters that occurred in Israel." Greapa hurriedly sent Joshua to Joseph, instructing him to keep yet one more seat open for them at Great Hall. The five of them then proceeded to discuss how to weave Moshe's speaking in with theirs.

As they prepared to leave for the gathering, Greapa ventured a query. "If I might ask you, sir, how is it you are here now, when the King commanded you to come this morning, which was but an hour or two ago?"

The response from the smiling Moshe should have been expected. "One of the King's servants brought me here, to the very outskirts of your small city. He pointed me toward your home, then left. At my time of need, he will bring me back to the King." Greapa understood the "servant" to be one of the King's many angels.

They walked to Great Hall, speaking as they went. The conversation of those walking nearby turned from animated to hushed when they observed the robe of the Israeli. The Levitical priests were only seen in and around Jerusalem. No one—at least no one of this town—had ever seen a priest outside of Israel. Minds spun trying to grasp the seriousness of what was happening, yet no one asked the quintet a single question. Seeing the priest in their town was shocking enough; speaking to him was out of the question.

As the fivesome entered the hall, the chatter of those who had preceded them hastily ended as heads turned to see the robed figure with Greapa and the others. Shock, disbelief, and even some dismay could be seen in the disquieted crowd. Anxious whispers passed one to another; looks of befuddlement were nearly ubiquitous.

Greapa began by thanking God and praising the King, to which Moshe gave a ringing, "Amen!" Looking to the priest, Greapa began, "This is Moshe, who has been sent to us by the King." The wide eyes around him somehow became even wider with this announcement. "He will address us in a short while. First, I would like to give a brief overview of where we are in our speaking.

"The United States had become greatly weakened. This emboldened China to invade the many islands of the Pacific Ocean, even going so far as northern Australia. A great persecution of Christians had broken out across the globe, with China being the greatest perpetrator of these monstrous evils. Indeed, persecution was nearly everywhere: in China, along both coasts of the United States, in Russia, in the ten-nation Mediterranean confederacy, in the continents to the south—then called Africa and South America—and in various other places."

"The world had come close to annihilation, but had stepped back. The emperor of the confederacy had managed to convince Israel and the Arab nations to agree to a treaty that seemed to give all peace, but actually allowed him to insert himself into the affairs of all those countries.

"A pact of about seven years had been signed and was about to be implemented . . . "

Moshe then stood and spoke with the authority of the One who sent him, "I am Moshe, sent by the King to relay to you the happenings in Israel as the previous age closed. I lived in Jerusalem during those years, practiced the religion of my ancestors, and was an apprentice architect by trade. Though I was young, the simplicity of my architectural designs was looked upon with favor by my seniors, and though I was not overly zealous, my firm belief in our religion was approved with pride by my teachers.

"Those years in Israel were very difficult. Terrorists from among the Muslim communities sought to harm, kill, and destroy us. We were much hated by them. At times they would even kill in the streets of the Beloved City. We sought peace amidst a people who abhorred us. Unfortunately—or perhaps I should say, most fortunately—the agreement of peace we eventually were offered turned out to be a great deception authored by the evil one, Satan.

"I did not know or believe in Jesus. He was most despised among the Jews at that time, especially among the most religious of us. Successive governments of Israel arduously sought to ban and exclude him from every part and facet of the country. This concerted effort to eliminate Christ from the minds and hearts of the people was highly successful, so much so that I knew very little about him. I never read his words in the Great Book; I never heard of his doings; I never knew of the beauty of his Being. But though he was loathed by many, I was not one of them—I simply did not know him.

"As the end approached, I was in Jerusalem learning and practicing my chosen trade. Israel had slowly been making peace with many of its neighbors. The extremists among the Arabs detested that peace and attempted to disrupt and destroy it using various means, but they did not succeed.

"Then that fateful day came. I was walking outside on the western outskirts of Jerusalem and saw many people pointing to the sky. As I turned to look in the direction they were pointing, I saw a fighter jet—a kind of extremely fast airplane—screaming across the sky heading towards Jerusalem. We did not understand what was happening. As it approached the city it seemed to adjust its course, apparently to head directly for the Temple Mount. There was nothing anyone could do to intervene and stop what was about to occur. As we looked on in horror, it crashed at incredible speed and full force into the mosque on top of the Mount.

"The airplane was, in fact, laden not only with a nearly full complement of highly flammable fuel but also explosive weapons, and as a consequence produced an enormous fireball as it collided with the mosque. As wreckage erupted outward, everything on the Mount's summit was devastated.

"The chaos and peril that ensued were unspeakable. Were it not for the threat of nuclear war, Israel almost certainly would have been overrun by hordes of crazed Muslims. The fact that it was a Muslim fanatic who destroyed the mosque, as we later learned, meant nothing. The deeply rooted hatred of Israel within many of the Arabs came to the fore, and there was seemingly no way to stop an all-out confrontation.

"But then that leader of the Mediterranean empire—that emperor—intervened to calm the situation while he attempted to work out a solution. I saw this leader; in fact, I met and spoke with him briefly. He had an outward charm that was seemingly irresistible. However, there was something hidden within him—something dark, something evil and calculating.

"He was joined by another cunning politician, a man of Israel. This malevolent man went to great lengths to promote both the emperor and the emperor's schemes. Between the two of them, they managed to convince a large majority of Israelis to vote to ratify an agreement which lasted approximately seven years—an agreement which, in my opinion, was extremely dangerous for Israel.

"Indeed, behind the scenes the emperor had promised the Arabs to betray Israel and let them swarm in and destroy it once Israel's military was completely neutralized. This fit precisely with the secret plans of the Arab countries, and it was by such assurances that he convinced the Arabs to ratify the agreement. Unknown to all, this duplicitous leader also planned to betray the Arabs. His hidden agenda was to overrun and conquer not only Israel but many Arab countries as well.

"After the treaty was ratified and the seven years of its term began, we immediately set out to clear the Temple Mount of debris and to restore the ground there to its proper condition. This took about nine months to accomplish; that is how severe the devastation was. We then set up the altar and commenced offering the evening and morning oblations, as was proper. The first item in the building of the Temple must be the altar with its sacrifices.

"The building of the Temple proper then started in earnest. I was enlisted to help with some of the complications that arose in the interior design work. The design itself had existed for millennia—it is in the Great Book. However, there was need of someone to interpret the more difficult design elements and then translate that into the actual building components.

"This construction took more than two and a half years. During this period we were nearly completely oblivious to the world situation and what was transpiring outside of Israel. We were focused on the building of the Temple, on the execution of the seven-year agreement, and on what many believed to finally be peace for Israel."

As Moshe proceeded with his chronicling of the events in Israel during the endtime, his listeners had gradually overcome their shock at seeing a man of such high stature in their midst. As a result, Greapa's continuation of this tale seemed natural: "While Israel was enjoying what it thought was peace, all around it and throughout the world there was chaos. Confusion seemed to reign on the Earth—confusion of everything proper. It was as if the universe had turned upside down, with what was good now called evil and what was evil now called good.

"In the Mediterranean empire, that foul emperor was consolidating his control over the populace and continuing to increase his power and the territory over which he reigned. The emperor had devised a machine that could 'think' in a sense. The machine had no life, but rather it had many minute parts working together to mimic human thought. It was incredibly fast and amazingly powerful. It could solve problems that humans could not. Using this machine, the emperor waged war against countries to the east and to the south. He expanded eastward into Turkey and purposed to invade and conquer Egypt and those countries along the southern edge of the Mediterranean. No one was able to stand against him because of the enormous advantage this machine provided him.

"The slaughter of Christians continued unabated, particularly in the areas controlled by China. Refugees flooded en masse from the Pacific islands and the European continent—and, in fact, from all over the world—to the United States, which had become a refuge for the persecuted."

Greama then picked up the thread. "In the United States there was a strange dichotomy. In some parts, most notably the West Coast and the Northeast, Christians and Christian morality was hated and scorned. In those areas lawlessness was extreme. All types of criminal behavior were tolerated by those who governed. These areas became a haven of lawlessness. However, in other parts of the country, particularly the center and south of the United States, Christ was loved and preached. The zeal for him and for the Great Book was extraordinary. During those days many converted to Christ, believing the gospel spoken to them and turning from their sinful pasts.

"Although I lived in the Northeast, I did not agree with what I saw transpiring in much of the populace. Some of my friends were Christians. The government, backed by a hate-filled populace, sought to force Christians, including my friends, into doing things that violated their consciences. They were scorned, despised, mal-treated, and abused in almost every way. Some were even jailed because they refused to accede to the government's sinful demands. I visited them in prison, and rather than condemn those who had condemned them, they rejoiced and prayed for those who were persecuting them.

"By a strange confluence of events, my father was sent by his company to oversee certain projects in the south of the United States. Our whole family moved southward a short time later. Looking back upon those events, I later realized that was actually divine providence. I am deeply—very deeply—grateful for the King's hidden working to move us when he did. It will become apparent why a little later."

Elizabeth joined Greama's speaking. "In Great Britain it was even more extreme. There was no real haven for the Christians. They seemed to be universally hated. The government did its best to muzzle them, to keep them from speaking the truth of the Great Book. But they continued anyway. Then a most strange thing happened."

Greapa then went on: "The Temple was nearing completion in Israel, when suddenly, without any notice, some of the Christians disappeared. Many Christians had been proclaiming that they all would be taken from the Earth, but that is not what happened—a *few* of them disappeared, but most remained behind. There were reports of a brief dazzling light, and then . . . " As Greapa spoke, a revelation struck him that was so intense it left him speechless and nearly breathless. He looked helplessly to Greama who could see, could read on her husband's face, his predicament and picked up the story where Greapa had stopped. His mind reeled, but Greapa knew, had no doubt whatsoever, what had happened to those Christians—he had seen it happen to Lord Faithful.

Regaining his composure, he looked to Greama, who was relieved to see her husband's recovery. She stopped, and Greapa began from where he had left off. He realized he would be repeating some of what Greama must have said while he was wordless, but it would not be harmful to do so. The repetition should actually be quite helpful to those who were hearing this for the first time. He continued, "Some reported seeing dazzling light as someone near them disappeared. This was astonishing, something never seen before in the history of man.

"Many Christians were not taken at that time, but rather left behind to pass through what was about to come upon the Earth. The dismay and soul-searching among them was intense. They spoke of these things openly and wondered how they could have been so wrong in their understanding. The leaders among them who had propagated the misconception that all Christians would be taken before the endtime upheavals had various reactions to this incredible event. Some simply repented for their grievous error, realizing that because of their wrong teachings they may have hindered and even prevented many of the sons of God from being prepared for that moment. Others offered excuses such as 'How was I to know?' or, 'It was a reasonable interpretation based on what the Book says.' Some went so far as to accuse God of being a deceiver. This latter proclamation came from the weakest of those leaders.

"The concocted nonsense that was propagated by the governments and those who broadcast the news was simply not believable. Some said these Christians had gone into hiding, a ridiculous theory since hundreds of thousands and perhaps even millions had disappeared at the same time. Others posited that beings from another planet in another solar system in the universe had transported them away—a ludicrous fable. The Christians on Earth knew, however, what had happened to them. There was great alarm among those left on Earth because they knew they would pass through the great cataclysms that were about to strike the Earth. Slowly, a few Christians at a time, they returned to their work of preparation. What else were they to do?

"By the time the middle of the seven-year pact approached, Christians had been extirpated from China, the Pacific islands, and various other areas around the world by having been murdered, driven out, or by fleeing the hatred and violence directed at them. Much of the Earth, save for the southern United States, was completely in the hands of darkness."

Moshe spoke next. "We had hoped to finish the building of the Temple in time for the Passover that fell near the middle of the seven years of the pact. We worked day and night with that in view, and as that deadline drew near, it was apparent that we would indeed complete the Temple in time for that feast. A great celebration was planned.

"By then the great orator, who convinced many to ratify the pact, had become the prime minister of Israel. Many had voted to elect him to that office, having been charmed and deceived by him and the agreement he supported. Many among the people speculated that perhaps he was the Messiah. Some began to declare that he was, that he brought about peace in Israel and ushered in a new golden age for it. This evil leader not only did not dissuade such talk, but nodded his agreement when he heard it.

"He then invited the emperor to Israel for that Passover and went so far as to publicly announce he would be giving the emperor a guided tour of the interior of the Temple. This was an outrage to many in Israel, especially to those who were religious—the interior of the Temple was not for Gentiles, only Jews, and the Holy of Holies within it was only for the high priest, who could enter it but once a year, and only then with the blood of a sacrifice.

"This put the entire religious community in Israel at odds with the prime minister. The group was large and extremely influential, wielding much power within the Israeli government. The loss of support from this faction threatened the prime minister's position as leader. Nevertheless, he continued with his plan, and the religious ones set about trying to thwart him. As the day drew near when the tour was to take place, the emperor arrived in Israel to great fanfare and acclaim. His visit and the tour of the Temple were being televised—shown on television—throughout much of the world. The emperor was a master of appearance and he always took every opportunity to aggrandize himself. He had ensured that this event and the celebration in Israel that he himself had brought about would be seen everywhere on Earth.

"Many celebrities were there to welcome him and lend their support. The emperor himself, in a supreme show of confidence and assurance, walked about without so much as a single bodyguard. It almost seemed as if he were daring anyone to try to do him harm.

"At the same time, over the weeks and months leading up to the completion and dedication of the Temple, within Israel something inexplicable was occurring. Many among the people began having strange dreams and seeing what they said were visions. The old men were dreaming of the Messiah descending out of the clouds from the sky with great glory. Young men were seeing visions of calamities striking Earth. In particular, some saw meteors streaking across the sky and producing great pillars of smoke as they struck the ground. To many, this seemed to be a sure sign of the coming of the Messiah.

"Then a number of great events happened in rapid succession, leaving us stupefied. First, as the prime minister and the emperor were approaching to tour the Temple, a number of us stood at a distance, watching. We were all greatly dismayed by what the prime minister and the emperor were doing. We saw them scale the steps to the Mount and begin to greet many of the dignitaries who were also there for the tour. They all were surrounded by Levitical priests dressed in their priestly garb and other non-specific personnel. They approached the altar where a priest was about to offer the morning sacrifice. Suddenly, that priest lunged at the emperor with the blade of the sacrifice in his hand. We watched with great consternation as the blade struck the emperor in his head and neck, severing the artery supplying blood to his brain. Though those around the emperor did all they could to staunch the flow of blood, it was far too late. The emperor lay there dead.

"As we looked on in utter disbelief, some great meteors streaked across the sky. These struck not far from Israel, producing great pillars of debris rising into the air. The Earth trembled from the collisions. The smoke spread across the sky, first blotting out the sun and then turning the moon, which was on the opposite horizon, blood red. To those of us who knew the prophecies in the Great Book, we realized that this had been foretold in the writings of Joel."

Greapa interjected, "What Moshe is describing was not a localized event. Rather, a large swarm of sizable meteors had struck the Earth. This initiated a cascading series of earthquakes that shook the whole Earth. The sky was ablaze with meteor trails, especially in that part of the Earth that was night.

"This perplexed those who studied the stars, because in spite of their great lenses they used to survey the heavens, they had not seen this swarm of meteors approaching. As they traced back the trajectories the meteors had followed, they discovered that this great swarm had come not from our own solar system, but from somewhere outside of it. All their great observing devices were directed to find objects imperiling the Earth that were within our solar system. These meteors came from without and so escaped detection."

Shaking his head at the remembrance of these events, Moshe went on: "While scientists—experts in a particular field of study— were analyzing the trajectories of the great meteors that had just struck Earth, another startling event occurred in Jerusalem. The great celebration that was planned for that Passover had drawn many Jews from across Israel. Among these were the ones who had been experiencing the dreams and visions. They witnessed the fulfillment of those dreams and visions, and being stunned by this, were then mysteriously gathered by a strange sound into one of the larger of the various parks then existing in Jerusalem.

"Upon arriving there, they found two ancient figures dressed in sackcloth who warned and exhorted them about the coming days. They were told to find shelter against the immediate threat that was to overtake the Earth, even though by that time the great danger had not yet been made known. They were also told to wait for the 'abomination of desolation'—spoken of by Daniel the prophet—to be set up in the holy place of the Temple. When that occurred they were to flee to the mountains to the north, where they would find a place of refuge prepared for them. They were warned to flee immediately and not turn back for anything; to do so would bring dire consequences. Although these two ancient men did not declare their own names, it was in some way apparent to all there that they were Moses and Elijah, who had somehow returned to Israel for those final days."

Both Greapa and Moshe were now standing, taking turns detailing the great and amazing events that accompanied the advent of the day of the Lord. Greapa resumed: "While these events shook Israel, scientists analyzed the information available to them and then turned their observation devices to look in the direction from which the meteors came. They discovered something far worse, far more dangerous, far more imperiling. Hurtling towards Earth was an even larger and denser group of meteors, some of which had diameters that had to be measured in kilometers. The largest was more than six kilometers across. The scientists worked feverishly to determine the points of impact of these incoming asteroids and the likely damage they would cause. The leaders of all countries on Earth then addressed their populaces with this message:

The conclusions of scientists based upon their astronomical observations are these:

1. The meteors that just struck Earth are but the precursor of a far more destructive assault.

2. A great cloud of meteors will strike Earth beginning in about a day.

3. The densest swarm of meteors will strike Earth first. It will be so dense as to light up even the night sky, turning it red, and

heat the atmosphere to the point that much of any exposed living matter on Earth, particularly plant life, will be greatly damaged or destroyed.

4. This will be followed by the most immense object striking the Pacific Ocean. The likely result of this will be the destruction of most of the sea life and ships in the Pacific. Additionally, huge waves—some over 400 meters in height—will demolish the coast along the rim of the Pacific. How far into the interior of the coastlines those huge waves will travel is unknown—scientists have never seen such an event before—but we do know that nearly all life in the coastal areas of the Pacific will be completely obliterated. In addition, coastal areas in the southern Atlantic Ocean (the name they used for that great sea to our west) and parts of its northern coastline will be inundated and destroyed. Furthermore, the heat from the passage of this huge mountain through the Earth's atmosphere and the huge earthquakes resulting from the collision of this object with the Earth will do untold destruction and probably cause the death of millions of people.

5. Then another large asteroid, somewhat smaller than the one striking the Pacific, will fall on the Himalayan Mountains (which was the greatest mountain range on Earth, spreading across the Asian continent). Scientists cannot calculate the amount of damage this will cause.

6. The result of all these will be a prolonged darkness over about a third of the Earth, accompanied by a probable 10°–20° drop in temperature worldwide.

"The whole world had been trapped—ensnared—and there was no way to escape. The panic that ensued after this announcement was unparalleled. In metropolis after metropolis, terrified citizens attempted in any way possible to escape the near certain doom that was about to befall them. Great violence broke out—theft, murder, rape. But, in the midst of such chaos an angel appeared in mid-heaven. It was seen by the whole Earth at the same time—a very perplexing conundrum to scientists. It announced,

'Fear God, and give him glory, because the hour of his judgment has come: and worship him who made the heaven and the Earth and sea and fountains of waters.' This helped bring some sanity and sobriety to Earth's population.

"Wherever possible, people sought refuge in underground shelters. The so-called folly of the Christians, for which they had been unmercifully mocked, now turned out to be salvation for many. They, along with the ones who had helped them and many others, entered into the refuges they had built. Everywhere people sought out caves or any other natural or man-made underground space. The terror was so intense that people called for the rocks and mountains to fall on them, to hide them from the wrath of God and Christ. The hearts of many failed due to the extreme fear.

"Christians prayed desperately for God's protection and keeping. Repentance for their lack of preparation and readiness abounded. Then this unimaginable judgment struck."

There was no need for anyone to speak. Before their eyes, the vision of what had occurred unfolded.

First, the great swarm of meteors passed through the atmosphere, superheating it. They watched as grasses throughout the Earth withered and died. The destructive cloud struck all across the Asian continent, causing untold damage and uncontrollable fires. Trees throughout Asia burned wildly, turning it into a blackened lifelessness.

Next, the largest asteroid passed through the atmosphere as a great burning mountain, falling into the Pacific Ocean. The heat alone from this bolide's passage through the air vaporized most everything beneath its course. They watched as it passed through the ocean water and struck the sea floor below. The Earth shook violently. Enormous tsunamis spread out from the point of impact. They not only obliterated the entire Pacific Rim, but traveled far inland, destroying everything in their path. Parts of the Atlantic coastline suffered a similar fate, as the shock of the asteroid's collision passed through the Earth to the point-of-impact's antipode.

Then another large asteroid shot across the sky and landed in the Himalayan mountains. Debris exploded upward, much of it settling down upon the many rivers that streamed from the mountain heights. Survivors came forth from shelters into stifling hot air, and in an attempt to cool themselves and assuage their thirst, drank from these rivers. Many died from those poisoned waters.

Finally, the huge amount of debris in the air blacked out the heavens over Asia, and after a short time caused a great drop in temperature, particularly in the more northern latitudes.

Even though Greapa, Moshe, and the others speaking had actually passed through these events, they were overwhelmed by the vision before them. As Greapa looked about, he saw the audience gasping and weeping and wagging their heads. He realized none of them, including himself, could bear anything more that evening. After the few minutes it took him to recover, he dismissed the meeting and sat. Everyone sat. Silently.

They walked back home in somber quietness. Eventually Greapa queried, "You will eat with us today, Moshe?"

"Yes," was the simple response.

5

GREAT TRIBULATION

As they returned, Benyamin and Elizabeth headed to their
accommodations. Greapa remarked, "Rest. Tonight will
be another difficult time." The couple smiled slightly in
acknowledgment and turned into their lodging.

Upon arriving at their house, Greapa and Greama found
Joseph waiting expectantly. Leaving Greama with Moshe in the
dining room, Greapa took Joseph to his bedroom. He opened the
closet and reaching up into the back of an upper shelf, he pulled
out something covered in an old cloth. From under the cloaking
cloth Greapa removed what looked to be an ancient brass box with
some kind of sealing wax around its cover. He explained to Joseph,
"I will need this tonight at our gathering, but I do not want anyone
to be distracted by it. So, on your way home, keep the box covered.
If anyone asks what you are carrying, say it is a gift. When you go
to the gathering tonight, put this box in a satchel with some fruit
covering it. Should you be asked about that, tell them only that it
is some fruit to eat during a break. Covering the small container
with the cloth again, he handed it to Joseph. Greapa escorted him
to the front door and, as Joseph was leaving, commanded, "Do not
open the box!"

Greama saw Joseph carry out the cloth-covered box. Looking
at Greapa discerningly she said, "So you have decided to finally

reveal what that is?" Greapa gazed at her as if he were considering the best way to respond, but remained silent.

Moshe watched curiously, and as they sat for their afternoon meal he spoke, "I have two questions to ask you, Greapa, and feel free to decline to answer. The first is, what happened to you in the middle of your speaking about the disappearance of the Christians? The second is, what is it the man who was just here—I believe his name is Joseph—was carrying away?"

Greapa stared at Moshe carefully. They both were about the same age, but Moshe enjoyed perhaps the highest status of any man on Earth. Greapa did not want to offend such a person in any way. He replied, "As I spoke about the disappearance of the Christians and how that disappearance was accompanied by a dazzling light, I realized that I too have seen that. Occasionally the one who rules our town, Lord Faithful, has gifted us the briefest of looks at the dazzling divine glory. I believe it was the same light, the same glory, seen in those Christians who vanished from the earth. The divine Being who was in them came forth and in a very real sense consumed all that they were, including their bodies—consumed them, but did not kill them. I do not know whether I am making sense in my speaking right now, but I believe what I am saying is true."

Moshe nodded his head very slowly, "I also believe this to be true. I have on occasion seen such glory—unbearably bright but also unbearably beautiful. The King and the sons always walk in glory, but we are veiled to much, perhaps most, of what they truly are. We simply cannot bear to look upon God."

"As for your second question," Greapa continued, "if I may, let me defer the full answer to that until this evening. I will say that he was taking away a very old brass box. As for its contents . . . " Greapa could see the mild disappointment in Greama's eyes as he once again did not explain to her what he had stowed away these many years.

The air was somber as they ate—the morning's visions still lingered. The other four at the table—Joshua, Sarah, Nathanael, and Mira—were visibly shaken. Even in the days before the King's return, the events they witnessed earlier that day were unprecedented. All of those who had been raised under the peace and beauty of the King's reign with the sons must be experiencing a soul-wrenching inward upheaval. Eventually Greapa ventured a mood-changing question, "Moshe, what is it like to be so close to the King?"

A great smile filled Moshe's face, as he beamed with the thought of his King, "His beauty . . . " As he began, tears filled his eyes and his words caught in his throat. He breathed deeply to recover himself, then began again, "His beauty is beyond speaking. In every matter, in every movement, even in the slightest of nuances, his kindness and gentleness are present in overflowing abundance. He is like an all-encompassing fragrance that far surpasses the sweetest of flowers and pulls ever so tenderly at the most sensitive and vulnerable of our heart strings, drawing us to come closer to him, to be more like him. His kingly gait is filled with majesty; his poise at all times is beyond elegant; his grace is more excellent than the finest of feasts." As he spoke, those at the table were slowly uplifted, brought from the profound shock of God's judgments to the heights of God's revelation of his own heart for man. "I wish, I desire, I yearn to be like him in every way. I have no words to convey such a Being as he is. Yet in all this there is something more than iron in him—a kind of remarkable, unbreakable strength, power, authority, and majesty. There is no questioning of his Person and his status. He commands in such a way that we follow—that we *must* follow—by virtue of who and what he is."

Words flowed from Moshe like a stream in the desert, assuaging the deep thirst of those around him and sweeping away the pains of the morning. Food was forgotten as Moshe described the indescribable King and his experience of being so close to him. "To this day I cannot say why he so blessed me by placing me so near to him. I am utterly undeserving of such an immense honor." Shaking his head as if to wake from a dream, Moshe looked about at his rapt listeners and the food lying uneaten before them. He smiled again, cheerfully, and announced, "Let us eat! Tonight's gathering will also be hard, so we need nourishment. "

Greapa and Greama sat in their bedroom. They had guided Moshe to a second, smaller guest room where he could rest briefly before joining them to discuss the evening's speaking. They were about to lie down for a short nap when Lord Faithful spoke to them. Once again he appeared behind them, and once again they turned to see him. "We must almost apologize for this morning's very difficult visions. We realized that these would be nearly unbearable, but it was necessary. We must do all we can to help those born in this age to realize the seriousness of things past and things future."

"It was indeed hard, even for those of us who passed through those times. Will what you show tonight be as troubling?" asked Greapa.

"Probably not quite so demanding. For the sake of the people's already deeply burdened hearts, we must omit some things, such as what the great horde was actually doing when it murdered so many as it crossed Asia toward Israel. Quite a few could not bear that; some might even find such evil to be completely unbelievable. It will be hard enough for them to accept what was done in Israel and the great slaughter of the end," replied the lord.

Greapa shuddered. "Then what we heard concerning that host as it swept across Asia was true." He and Greama looked ill, their faces pale and sickly.

"Sadly, yes. The depravity of man when he is apart from God and under the influence of Satan is seemingly endless. But rest now. You have done remarkably well. Your reward will be great when you see how many of your kin, friends, and neighbors will be saved through your words." With that, Lord Faithful vanished.

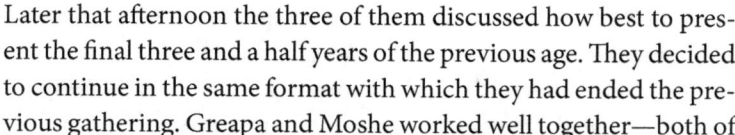

Later that afternoon the three of them discussed how best to present the final three and a half years of the previous age. They decided to continue in the same format with which they had ended the previous gathering. Greapa and Moshe worked well together—both of them would stand and take turns speaking, alternating between the global situation and what was happening in Israel. Greapa would address the worldwide happenings, while Moshe would speak to the crucial aspects of what happened in Israel. Greama, Benyamin, and Elizabeth would interject their personal experience at the appropriate times.

When Benyamin and Elizabeth arrived for dinner—they had once again been invited—Greapa explained how they were going to proceed. Benyamin and Elizabeth then spent some time considering and piecing together their experiences as the age closed.

As they ate at the table, Greapa related their interaction with Lord Faithful earlier that afternoon. However, he did not speak about the Asian horde because the four younger ones—younger at least relatively speaking—might not be able to bear the additional distress. Seeing an unparalleled opportunity before them—indeed, who had ever had a Levitical priest sitting at his dinner table, never mind one who served the King directly—Greapa posed another question to Moshe, "What are your duties in your service to the King?"

Moshe looked up from his plate, and while still chewing the tasty morsel he had just taken into his mouth, he peered at Greapa with searching yet gentle eyes. He then understood what Greapa was doing, and he agreed with it. This was not the age for secrets, but for an open display and communication of all that God and the King are and do. He smiled knowingly at Greapa, then answered, "My duties are many and varied. While there are some simpler tasks in the care for the Temple and the quarters of the priests, most of my responsibilities lie in the care for others. Jesus has a great heart—an immense heart. He is always caring for the things of God, caring for the people of God. We follow his lead in these matters. As you have seen, he has been turning the whole Earth into a paradise, starting from Israel and expanding outward. It is our main duty to communicate the joy of living before him—before God—to the people. In our case, we are intermediaries between him and the people of Israel. It is then for them, in turn, to communicate that to the people of Earth. God flows into Christ,

Christ flows into us, we in turn flow into Israel, and Israel flows to all the peoples. In this way, God supplies the whole Earth. Although he certainly could supply everyone directly, he chooses to communicate to all through others, and in so doing builds up love, trust, and kindness among us all. His ways are truly remarkable." As he looked around the table he saw a spellbound audience, once again with the food on their plates nearly untouched. With a smile he gave a gesture to the plates as if to say, "Eat!"

"You are much blessed," ventured Elizabeth.

"Indeed," replied Moshe, "we all are much blessed! Considering from where we came . . . " He looked to his left, seemingly looking back in time. He then spoke with somewhat choked words, "Considering from where we came, the blessings we now enjoy are beyond speaking."

They took their seats at the evening gathering and surveyed those surrounding them. Most, if not all, had recovered from the shock of the morning visions. There were color and robustness in their faces. They were indeed a strong people, able to bear the seemingly unbearable.

Greapa pondered something briefly and came to a decision. He stood and walked over to Greama and then, stooping down, whispered in her ear, "I will need you to come to the front near the end of the speaking."

As he walked back to his seat, she stared at him with surprise and wondered, *What is he planning?*

When those within the hall were settled and the throng outside had quieted, Greapa stood. He exclaimed loudly in his great, uplifting voice, "This night I praise the King! I praise our God! I thank him for all his servants. I thank him for bringing us to this point." Although there was more to be said in praise and thanks, Greapa simply let his words hang in the air and touch the hearts of those about him.

"Most of the speaking tonight will be done by Moshe and myself," Greapa said. "When it is appropriate Benyamin, Elizabeth, and Greama will add something of their experience during those troubling times. We will start by telling you what we went through as those first calamities struck."

Benyamin stood. "I was in Turkey, still at my uncle's orchard. I saw those first brilliant meteors streak across the sky. I saw the resultant columns of smoke rising. The Earth convulsed as earthquake after earthquake ensued. Not long after that we heard the announcement of the impending cataclysms. It was extremely difficult not to panic.

On my uncle's property was a large underground cavern in which he stored wine and other food supplies. How serendipitous! Our whole family worked together to remove all the glass and other dangerous objects from that shelter, and then with some friends we gathered in the cavern to await the coming judgment. We sat there in terror for hours, praying to a God we did not know and about whom we never much cared, pleading for mercy and help. Unlike what we all saw this morning, in that cavern we could not see what was happening outside, but we could feel the upheavals. As the first of these reached Turkey, the electricity stopped and, with that, our lighting. We lit the lanterns we had—similar to those we have now—in order to see.

"The cavern where we sheltered swayed and shuddered violently. Whether it was extremely sturdy or God heard our prayers, or both—I cannot say—we survived. As quake after quake passed through Turkey, the women with us screamed, the men held them, and we all cried out to that unknown God. We later learned that Turkey had been spared the most severe of the cataclysms." The anguish on Benyamin's face as he recalled the great trauma of those events was met by tears in the eyes of the audience.

Elizabeth then related her experience. "My elderly grandmother lived close to the Mediterranean Sea, to the west of where we are now. She was ill and in need of care. Although we were poor, my parents sent me to help her in her need. It was while I was there with her that the first meteors struck. When we heard the announcement of what awaited us in but a day's time, my grand-mother knew exactly what to do. She had been in the service of the government throughout most of her life. One of her various responsibilities was overseeing the care of underground bunkers that had been used for shelter during a previous great war that had engulfed the world. She had numerous friends in that branch of the government, whom she contacted. They allotted us spots in a bunker, which we hoped would provide safety from the incoming barrage. We gathered a few things that were critical, such as her medication, and then immediately fled to the shelter to which we were assigned. It was very close to us; otherwise it is unlikely we would have arrived in time, as the streets were filled with panicked people, many of whom had nowhere to go.

"When we arrived, guards armed with modern weapons stood at the bunker entrance, prohibiting entry to all but those who had been allotted places in the underground shelter. It was simply terrifying. In one day's time the world as we knew it would come to an end, and we all might be dead. Within the shelter men and women were weeping; many of them were crying out to a God they once cursed. Some were in such a state of panicked terror that they cried out for the rocks and mountains to fall on them. The day of judgment—a day which none of us believed would ever occur—had come.

"We knew exactly when the great rocks from the sky would hit. That had been part of the announcement. But we would not feel the effects of those impacts until sometime later. It would take hours for the shock of those collisions to reach us. The time came and, as expected, we felt nothing. We waited and prayed, hoping to somehow survive. Finally the waves of shock from those impacts struck us.

"The first ones jostled us considerably, but as it turned out these were minor compared to what we were about to experience. Children and women were crying and screaming. Even the men wept. There were a few brave souls who tried to calm others in between the quakes. They would talk soothingly in a gentle voice or sing, hoping to get others to join in—but as soon as the next quake hit, the chaos resumed.

"This went on for hour after hour until the largest of all the upheavals hit. There was no one and no thing left standing. We were bounced off walls, the ceiling, the floor, and each other. Thankfully, furniture was bolted down and everything made of glass, or in some other way dangerous, had been removed from the shelter in anticipation of just such an event. Many people were injured, some severely. Broken bones, lacerations, and contusions were widespread.

"This went on for a full day, then the huge earthquakes subsided. There were many aftershocks that shook us and rekindled the fear that something worse was about to happen, but nothing did. Somehow, we made it through without a single fatality. There were many injuries but no one died. We later discovered that the area we were in was actually not hit hard.

Elizabeth stopped speaking, then Greama followed. "As I mentioned previously, my family had moved to the southern United States some time before the asteroid swarm struck Earth. My father's main responsibilities for his job related to the construction of many of the underground shelters being built by Christians and others. A number of the younger Christians were my friends. I listened to their speaking about Jesus, but for some reason I was not touched in the same way they were. When many Christians— some of whom I knew—suddenly disappeared, it moved me to take the talk about Jesus much more seriously. But the end came quickly after that.

"My father did not accept the talk of the end as being true, but to him it was his responsibility to construct what his customers wanted, not to question the veracity of their motives. But he was also a wise man: he made sure there was space for his whole family in one of the numerous shelters he had built, in case what the Christians were saying was true. When those first rocks struck, earthquakes rocked the whole Earth. We thought that perhaps the Christians were correct, and so headed immediately for that underground bunker where my father had secured space for us.

As we drove to that shelter, we had to contend with many impediments that were caused by the earthquakes. We then heard the announcement of the incoming cloud of meteors and giant asteroids over one of the long-distance listening devices—called 'radios'—that were common in those days. We also saw the angel in mid-heaven proclaiming God's judgment was at hand.

"In the shelter, the four of us were joined by sixteen others. There was enough food, water, and supplies there for the twenty of us for a number of months. The Christians had planned well. We hoped that by the time we were able to come forth from the shelter, the situation outside would allow us to grow the food we needed to live.

"Within that little shelter we all prayed. My family and I believed there was a God. However, we did not have the same belief about Jesus as the others did. But we could and did pray together with them. We prayed for safety not only for ourselves but for the whole human race. The Christians there prayed with tears streaming down their faces, yet they were calm. In the midst of such an incredible catastrophe, they had an inexplicable peace.

"We were quite a distance away from nearly all the impact sites, so it was some time before the effects of those strikes reached us. When they finally did, it was quite violent. The upheavals lasted for many hours. At times we were tossed about like paper in a windstorm. I was quite bruised and shaken, but otherwise okay. My father and a few of the Christians suffered more serious injuries. We tended to them as best we could as we suffered quake after quake, and shaking upon shaking.

"The structure in which we hid was well built. It did not collapse or experience any serious damage. It had been constructed to withstand extreme shock, and divine providence assured that it did. One of its features was a means to view what was happening outside from within it. At first the sky lit up with meteor after meteor streaking across it. The heavens turned bright blood red from the heat of all these passing through the atmosphere and from the molten particles erupting into the sky from the numerous impacts of the meteors. We could not see how any living creature above ground could survive such heat—at least in the area where we were.

"The atmosphere stayed red-hot for some time and then slowly darkened as the debris in the air cooled. Eventually the sky was veiled by a thick haze, which lingered for months and dropped the air temperature significantly."

Moshe then rose to speak. "On the Temple Mount where I was, there was pandemonium—utter chaos. Between the slaying of the emperor, the impacts of those first meteors, and the resulting tremors, complete confusion overran us all. Some were running in various directions; others walked aimlessly. Some just stood, stunned at the events that had taken place. The emperor still lay where he had fallen, although he had been covered with a cloth or blanket of some sort. He had been there more than an hour—the turmoil of events had interrupted all action to remove him. However, there was no doubt that he was dead. He had not moved in all that time, and blood had long since stopped flowing from his grievous wound.

"To our even greater shock, the cloth covering the emperor started to move, and before all our eyes—indeed, before the eyes of all those who were still able to watch television—he suddenly stood on his feet. Before our very eyes we saw his wound heal itself. Looking around to all the astonished priests and dignitaries, he declared, 'I am God. I cannot be killed.' He then walked into the Temple, proclaiming himself to be God.

"We tried to grasp the happenings unfolding around us, but we were dazed. We seemed to be in a dense fog, groping for something to steady ourselves. How long we were in that state I do not know. Then one of those in charge of the tour, or perhaps it was one of the priests—I was too bewildered to distinguish between people—started shaking us and telling us to go below to the shelters. I stumbled my way into one of the underground caverns beneath the Mount. It was only then that I learned of the great cataclysms about to take place.

"We prayed. We prayed in the way we had been taught. It was as if we were in some kind of dream—or rather, some kind of nightmare. Nothing seemed real. Time passed, but I was too bewildered to take notice. We had some supplies in those caverns, but we did not know the extent of them or how much would be needed.

"The effects of those great impacts finally reached us, but there and in that whole region they were not severe. Israel had been spared extreme damage. We did not know what was in store for us, however."

As Greapa rose, Moshe remained standing. They would be speaking in turn for a good while, and they felt it better to not distract the listeners by frequent up and down movements. Greapa spoke of his experience briefly. They too had underground shelters on his father's vineyard, which were amply supplied. They too had prayed. They too were shaken, although not to the extremes others experienced.

Greapa then addressed the consequences of God's judgment upon the world. "The aftermath of these asteroid strikes was unimaginable. The Earth was scorched everywhere. Volcanoes were erupting. Great wave after great wave struck shorelines." As Greapa spoke, the transfixed audience saw—literally *saw*—that about which he was speaking. Before their eyes a vision from the past appeared, while Greapa acted as narrator. "Asia was most severely damaged. Trees, shrubs, and grasses burned in an enormous, uncontrollable wildfire. Rivers and streams were poisoned. Asia's Pacific Ocean coastline was completely obliterated. All those islands in the Pacific that China had conquered were simply gone, and China's immense navy no longer existed. Great cracks had appeared in the Earth's crust. Rivers of molten lava flowed in various places. The sky above Asia was completely blackened—no light from sun or moon shined through. Those who managed to survive that incredible catastrophe were forced to stay underground for months. The air above was toxic; the temperatures were too cold to be habitable; food supplies were non-existent." To all Greapa's listeners, who only knew the lush, luxurious, and multihued flora of their present age, the vision was overwhelming.

Greapa went on, "The entire coast of the great Pacific Ocean for hundreds of miles inland was totally annihilated—nothing remained alive. The eastern coast of Asia, the northern coast of Australia, all the islands in the Pacific, and the western coasts of the Americas were gone—simply *gone*. So many great and immense cities simply ceased to be, in what was only a matter of moments. Much of the coast of the Atlantic Ocean also suffered tremendous damage—the eastern part of South America, the west coast of Africa, and the northeast coast of North America all were virtually destroyed."

Greapa paused to let his listeners catch their breath. The vision stopped for the time being. He took a drink of water, and considered his next words. Upon seeing color returning to the faces around him, he continued, "Inland, many areas remained somewhat intact, although they had been greatly shaken by the tremendous earthquakes that had accompanied the great meteor impacts. In most areas the survivors were forced to remain underground for weeks. In the southern United States, the many Christians who lived in that area, along with those who had fled persecution, were somewhat ready for this extreme and dire emergency. They were accompanied by many non-Christians who had helped prepare for this time—ones such as Greama." He turned to her and nodded with a grim smile. None of them enjoyed reliving that time, but for the sake of their many offspring it was crucial that they did.

"When the survivors came forth from their subterranean dens, they found an Earth barely, if at all, habitable. The amount of sunlight, the temperatures, the toxicity of air and soil all combined to make farming extremely difficult. While many had supplies to last some months, it was questionable whether they would be able to survive long enough for the land to produce food.

"Much of what was left above ground had been too damaged to be serviceable, and what was not damaged was not functional—all the farming equipment was useless because there was no fuel. All the devices used to communicate and accomplish daily tasks were useless—not only was there no electricity, there was no hope of electricity being restored in the future. All the means of transportation were useless—again, there was no fuel. The whole world as man knew it had come to an end.

"Except . . . *except* in the continent we are now on, in Israel and the Middle East, and around the Mediterranean Sea. Strangely, these areas passed through this upheaval largely unscathed. When we emerged from our shelters, most buildings were intact. There was damage, but it was mostly superficial. There was no electricity, but after not too long it was partly restored."

Moshe recognized his cue. "In Israel we exited our shelters within a few days to a largely intact environment. There was some damage, but for the most part it was minor. The air smelled of burnt ash and the sun was dim in the sky. It was quite chilly for that time of year, more like winter than springtime. Electricity was sporadic, as were communications to other parts of the world. We slowly learned of the horrendous disasters in Asia, the Americas, and elsewhere. The great powers that had ruled the Earth and directed the path of mankind—China, Russia, and the United States—had been completely neutralized. Israel and the Mediterranean had become the center of the Earth.

"The prime minister of Israel took that opportunity to declare martial law: the military, rather than civil authorities, would rule the country. In this case, since our military had been effectively abandoned, it was the emperor's forces that took control under the direction of the prime minister.

"Each member of the emperor's military bore a mark with a tiny device attached to their foreheads or right hand. The mark bore the name of the emperor or the number 666, the number he himself had designated. The tiny device allowed them to communicate with each other and with another extremely powerful device—a kind of ultra-fast computer—that could direct and coordinate their movements, suggest courses of action, display imagery within their minds, and even control them if *it* so chose.

"During the first half of the seven-year pact, these forces acted properly and leniently with the people of Israel. However, after the slaying of the emperor and the great catastrophes, they became increasingly belligerent. At times they appeared to be in a trance, as if they were being controlled by an outside force. We became quite wary of them and the devices with which they were branded.

Moshe continued his description. "The emperor made his way back to his capital city, but with the help of the prime minister—and using the attempt on his life as justification—he first abolished the offerings on the altar before the Temple. In fact, he did away with the entire Levitical priesthood. He also stated he would return in due time.

"In the emperor's absence, and at his command, the prime minister ruled ruthlessly. He became harsh and even violent. With Israel's military disbanded and the emperor's forces under his control, he could do whatever he pleased. There was no way for us to fight against him. He began to strongly urge the citizens of Israel to receive the same mark as the emperor's military, stating that this would guarantee obedient behavior in that time of urgency. He became progressively more forceful in this matter.

"Many in Israel, particularly those who supported the prime minister, quickly and even happily acceded to his demands. But a good number of us refused. We did not agree with handing the control of our beings over to what we saw as a shadowy, hidden, and sinister force of some kind.

"The prime minister gradually eliminated all opposition to him in the Israeli government. A number of officials died in 'accidents.' Many resigned their positions under duress. Others simply disappeared. When the opposition was eradicated, the prime minister assumed the position of a dictator, just as the emperor had done in his empire.

"Then, when he saw that many were refusing his injunction to receive the emperor's mark, he took a further step. He declared that only those with the mark could buy and sell. He was able to do this because by that time the great and powerful device, to which all those bearing the mark were connected, controlled all buying and selling. This made it extremely difficult to obtain food and other necessities. We were despised by the many who bowed the knee to the emperor and his accomplice, the prime minister—but still we refused that mark."

Moshe looked to Greapa, who judged the time to be right for a brief pause and conveyed that to those at the meeting. He sat with Moshe, and beckoned to Joseph for some of the food Joseph had brought to cover that mysterious box. They simply sat, ate some fruit, and relaxed for a time, until the atmosphere seemed proper to continue.

As the people seated themselves and quieted, Greama stood first to speak. "On the other side of the Earth, we were in our shelter—in what was left of the United States—for a number of weeks, waiting for the dust in the atmosphere to settle and for the temperature to become somewhat hospitable. There were numerous tremors occurring daily as the Earth reverberated from the shock of those asteroid impacts. Some of us were hurt quite seriously. My father was one of those. While we had some medical supplies, we did not have the facilities or the expertise needed to help those who had been injured internally. When we finally exited our shelter, my father and one other were near death. There was nothing we could do for them except pray, for all the medical facilities were destroyed or shut down. Most of the housing around us was now rubble. There was no electricity and there were no means of travel. Roads and pathways bore great cracks from the earthquakes. Even if we could find a vehicle that had somehow remained intact, fuel for our vehicles was greatly limited. However, we did have a supply of medication to ease the pain of those who were suffering. My mother and I held my father in our arms as he died." Greama spoke now with tears in her eyes. Her distress as she relived those moments was evident. "I prayed that God would remember all my father had done for the Christians, when the time came that he stood before him. The other one who was seriously injured— a man named John—also died about that same time. We buried them both near our shelter."

She paused to gather herself and the strength needed to continue, then started anew. "There were a number of other shelters not far from us. We set about contacting their survivors. With them we began the great task of survival that was before us. We pooled our resources: those with expertise in certain critical areas—agriculture, medicine, architecture, construction, and so many others—arranged work groups to start taking care of those areas critical to our well-being.

While we did not have electricity, we did have a human-powered machine that could generate enough electricity to power the communication device we had stored in our shelter. We were able to contact others who were in a predicament similar to ours. Together we started to work out long-range plans for our future.

Elizabeth and Benyamin then spoke briefly in turn. Great Britain was in dire shape. Those there had not constructed many shelters like those in the United States had. Many had died, even though that area had not been subjected to direct strikes from the asteroid swarm. The heated atmosphere, the huge tsunamis and accompanying waves, the earthquakes, and the general turmoil from those disasters had taken their toll on human life. Subsisting there would be even more difficult than in the southern United States. Turkey, on the other hand, had fared comparatively well. Like Israel, the quakes and other catastrophes there were relatively minor.

Greapa then stood with Moshe at his side and spoke, "The area around the Mediterranean, including where we now are, was spared the greatest of that devastation, as were Israel and the whole of the Middle East. The rest of the Earth, with a few notable exceptions, was nearly completely destroyed. The world that people had known was gone, destroyed by the wrath of God in one severe judgment. In Asia alone we estimate more than a billion people died in but a few days. Along the Pacific Rim hundreds of millions more died. The death toll worldwide was unthinkable.

"The emperor returned from Israel a short time after these cataclysms. He moved quickly to consolidate his power and to manage the damage throughout his empire. While the destruction within the countries of his domain was minimal, nearly all the foreign sources of goods and produce no longer existed. All these had to be replaced by sources either local or from around the Mediterranean.

"His military controlled everything. Furthermore, there was enormous pressure to receive that evil person's mark with its mind-controlling internal device. Many of us refused. Thankfully, we lived on a vineyard in a rural area and were not subjected to much scrutiny. Then the dictum from the emperor came forth limiting buying and selling to those who bore his mark. However, we were able to survive by trading goods and services with other nearby farms and ranches. The emperor believed he could control everything, but many of us slipped through his fingers like water through a cupped hand.

"With the overseas sources of goods eliminated, internal replacements had to be developed. Surprisingly, this took place quickly. Within a year's time, trade within the empire was flourishing. While travel and transportation by airplane was greatly limited due to the amount of debris still in the air and the general lack of the specialized fuel needed for these planes, sea-going transports and trade abounded. The whole empire under the rule of the emperor's iron fist entered what seemed to be a peculiar and eerie Golden Age. The emperor's capital—Rome—experienced a renaissance, a kind of rebirth. Costly goods of all sorts flowed into the city, enriching its populace and government.

"However, in the midst of this, the hatred toward Christians and Jews increased dramatically. Their places of worship were subjected to ever-growing vandalism and destruction. Eventually, in one night all the houses of worship, particularly of the greatest of all their religions—called Roman Catholicism, were burnt to the ground. Its headquarters, which was situated in a section of Rome itself, was utterly destroyed at that same time. Its leader—called the Pope—was murdered, along with all his subordinates. The emperor had effectively rid himself and his empire of religion.

"To escape this slaughter, many of the Christians and Jews went into hiding. We helped a number of them hide. I recalled what that angel had said when the asteroid swarm was about to strike Earth: *Fear God*. I took those words to heart. We fed them, clothed them, and met their other needs. I believe Greama, Benyamin, and Elizabeth all had similar experiences." The eyes of the audience turned to each of these three, who were nodding their heads in agreement with Greapa.

"The situation in Israel," continued Moshe, "became progressively worse. The prime-minister-turned-dictator used increasing force to bring the whole country under his control. Word got out that the emperor was planning to return. In honor of the emperor, the prime minister erected an image of him in the Temple. However, this was no ordinary image. Within it were various minute devices powered by electricity. It was connected to that extremely 'intelligent' computer that Greapa has previously mentioned.

"This image could talk and recognize human speech. It could see its surroundings and actually move about. Furthermore, it was in the form of the emperor. It was as if the emperor himself were sitting in the inner chamber of the Temple, passing judgment on all those who were brought before it.

"This image controlled the emperor's army in Israel through those devices implanted with the emperor's mark. At the prime minister's behest, the emperor's military forces were instructed to coerce everyone in Israel to receive the mark. These forces bore a kind of armor that enabled them to have what appeared to be superhuman power and abilities. For example, they could climb up buildings and see through walls. Their strength was phenomenal. They carried a weapon that broadcast a kind of invisible wave. When that wave touched people, it caused excruciating pain. These weapons did not kill, they simply caused indescribable torment. They used these weapons in an attempt to coerce us to receive the emperor's mark.

"There seemed to be no way to escape, except to accede to the prime minister's demands. I can recall"—Moshe shuddered as he spoke—"the screams of my fellows as they were stung by this weapon. I can recall myself being stung. It was like my whole body was on fire, like every single nerve in my body was being ruthlessly burned. We wanted to die because the pain was so intense, and yet we could not. Death escaped us.

"Perhaps the most frightening thing of all was the look upon the faces of the emperor's military during this torment. There was a sinister gleam in their eyes and a devilish glee as they tortured us. We asked for mercy, but they laughed and persecuted us all the more. They seemed to be something other than human; they seemed to be just like that image that sat in the Temple. It seemed that another life—another *being*—was living within them and speaking through them. I never believed in demons until I saw the faces of these tormentors.

"This agony went on for five months, although it seemed like five years. By the time it ended we were worn out, exhausted, ready to do almost anything. But still we resisted. We still refused the emperor's mark.

"Having failed to coerce us to follow his commands regarding the mark, the prime minister then decreed that all those without it would be subject to death or exile. As people were taken to that vile image, it commanded them to be killed or sold as slaves to foreigners.

"Then the emperor returned to Israel. He flew there in a plane that was piloted remotely by his image! Upon his arrival he was astounded to find that not only had many in Israel refused his mark, but that tens of thousands of Jews were passing through the Holy Land, speaking of the coming of Christ and announcing Jesus' return in glory. These had appeared seemingly out of nowhere immediately after the five months of torment ended. As I found out later, they were the same Jews who had been drawn to Moses and Elijah in Jerusalem shortly after the first asteroids struck. They had fled to the mountains when the prime minister erected the image of the emperor in the Temple. They had then returned to help lead Israel back to God. While they passed through the cities of Israel, Moses and Elijah were doing great signs: shutting the heavens so it did not rain, calling down fire out of heaven upon their enemies, and other remarkable things.

"The emperor and the prime minister belittled the doings of those two; they mocked their clothing (for they were dressed in sackcloth) and criticized their speech as absurd. They went so far as to say the signs they were doing were trifles. To prove their point, as he stood before the emperor, the prime minister also called down fire out of heaven!

"The hatred of God and Christ by the emperor and prime minister drove them to turn many of their resources toward finding and exterminating the two witnesses for Christ and their army of preachers. The emperor himself had gone to the south to further expand his empire, leaving the prime minister and the abominable image in the Temple to deal with those who were not yet under the image's control. By ones, twos, threes, and more, these preachers were captured and brought before the emperor's image. The image commanded many of these to be beheaded. Others it either sent to torture in prison or exiled to foreign lands as slaves. Even though their numbers were being quickly diminished, they continued to preach, going from city to city in Israel. At the same time, the two ancient ones brought plague after plague upon the Earth in the hope of bringing man to repentance."

Greapa then spoke concerning the worldwide situation. "In the United States, the survivors in the southern areas had banded together into groups. While survival was both difficult and paramount, the foresight of many—combined with the expertise of the southern farmers and ranchers—had provided a means to supply the most critical need of food. Among the survivors of the great upheaval were doctors and nurses, who tended to the sick as best they could, given the great lack of medical facilities. The underground shelters provided protection as needed from the various adverse atmospheric phenomena they faced during those days.

"These mainly Christian groups slowly melded into sweet Christ-seeking communities. Doctrinal differences were put aside and religious practices were forgotten. They repented and prayed together with tears; they worked together with hymns and songs; they met together with longing for their Lord; they praised with joy. In all these communities the imminent return of the One they loved provided hope and motivation to continue on. While not all were so diligent in following their Lord, most were.

"However, they heard of impending danger of great import. Word had gone out from them concerning their welfare and progress. Some survivors had headed south in an attempt to join with the Christian communities there. But many survivors from other areas around the United States, chiefly from the West, had banded together to form a kind of marauding army. As they passed eastward in search of food and other supplies, they raided every place in their path, murdering many people in the process. When they heard of the situation in the South, they determined to sweep into that area, kill the people there, and steal the foodstuffs and other supplies on which the Christians and others were surviving.

"Great prayer went up to God, reminding him of his word—his promises—in the Great Book. In answer, miraculously, a tremendous earthquake struck the marauding army as it approached the South. They were swallowed up by a vengeful Earth.

"In Asia there were many survivors of the upheaval. With an initial population of billions, it was not surprising that hundreds of millions remained. These were ruthless, merciless, cruel, and bloodthirsty. They formed into numerous immense armies and headed westward across Asia, slaughtering everything and everyone in their path." The vision of these enormous armies played before the listeners. Awestruck eyes widened and mouths gaped. What they were seeing seemed simply inconceivable. "There were 200 million of them streaming toward Israel. We estimate that along their route they killed about a third of mankind. This is how vicious they were. They reached a great river, called the Euphrates, and paused there, as they determined by what means they could cross it.

"Furthermore, to the far north the Russian army was preparing to invade the Middle East, destroy the emperor, and plunder his empire. This had been well planned by Russia long in advance—destroy Israel and all the Arab nations along with the emperor, and pillage all the wealth accumulated there. As the armies from the East advanced upon Israel, the Russian armies advanced southward.

"Nearly all of the marauders rode horses; there was a dearth of fuel for powering man-made vehicles, and the roads on which the vehicles operated had been nearly totally destroyed by the great upheavals. They all were being drawn to Israel as if by some intense magnet. They had no idea what the future held for them.

Moshe joined in to bring the narrative to a near climax. "The emperor heard of these approaching forces and returned to Israel with great wrath, determined to demolish all these incoming armies and put an end to the Israeli opposition—in particular, to the two ancient ones and their followers. He planted his tents on a long plain between Jerusalem and the Mediterranean. After ordering his forces, he then set about eliminating the so-called 'holy people'—the two ancients and their followers.

"By that time there were very few of the Jewish preachers left; they had been systematically eliminated by the prime minister, using the forces the emperor had left behind in Israel. As the last of these preachers proclaimed the coming of Christ in the final cities of Israel to hear this announcement, they were met by the emperor and his forces. He slaughtered them quickly and without fanfare. He and the prime minister then came face to face with the two ancient ones—Moses and Elijah—in Jerusalem.

"Those two great leaders of Israel could have called down fire to consume the emperor. They could have struck them with any number of plagues. They could have commanded the Earth to swallow them whole. But to our amazement they did nothing. We had hoped that perhaps they would have some way to deliver us from the certain destruction we faced, but they did *nothing!* They allowed themselves to be killed. The emperor oversaw their murder, and then proclaimed a feast with days of rejoicing for, as he said, 'These two ancients have tormented us all for far too long.'

"The bodies of Moses and Elijah lay dead in the street for days. Nobody touched them. Their deaths were televised throughout the empire. People rejoiced greatly. They even sent presents to one another, celebrating the murder of these two holy ones. The power of the holy people had finally been broken and the holy people crushed.

"We were in the utmost despair. Our country was filled with the emperor's vicious armies, millions of murderous forces were at the Euphrates about to overflow into Israel, Russian armies were in the mountains north of Israel also intending to destroy us, and what we saw as our last hope—Moses and Elijah—lay dead before us in Jerusalem. We wept in our desolation and hopelessness."

Greapa looked about, saw the entranced listeners, and said, "We are going to stop here for the night." The audience was too stunned at his interruption to complain. He went on, "But before we go, there is one more thing." He looked to Joseph, who recognized Greapa's request and reached under his chair to open the fruit-laden satchel, pulled out the cloth-covered ancient box, and handed it to Greapa.

Greapa held the box up and removed the cloth. The ageless brass container still showed a bit of a gleam beneath its heavy patina. He then turned to Greama and said, "Dear wife, would you come here to help me?" Greama smiled at her secretive husband, nodded her assent, and came forward. Greapa pulled a small knife from his pocket and handed both the box and the knife to Greama. He said to his rapt listeners, "This box and its contents are nearly as old as I am. I have kept them safe these many centuries for just such an occasion as this. Even Greama does not know what the contents are. And my dear wife has never pried or nagged me about it, though she has seen it in my possession all these years. I think it most fitting that she now break the seal of this box and reveal its contents."

With a somewhat shocked and bewildered expression, Greama whispered in her husband's ear, "You rascal!" She started to cut through the seal around the rim of the container. When she finished, she handed the knife back to Greapa and slowly wriggled the top off the box. She looked inside quizzically, and first pulled out a brass-clad jeweler's loupe, which would be immediately recognizable to all of her day. She examined it, held it up for all to see, then handed it to Greapa. She then again looked into the box and stared within with great interest. She looked, then looked again more closely, then smiled. She delicately removed a small rectangular object from the box as if she were taking a baby from a cradle, and examined it carefully. She look at Greapa, and struggling to hold back tears, she buried her head in his shoulder. After regaining her composure, she looked back to Greapa, who gave her a slight nod of assent. She walked over to Moshe and handed him the object.

Moshe turned to Greapa, and seeing the agreement in his face, took the object carefully. He scanned it, then scanned again, moving his head back and forth as if he were reading. He smiled broadly, then squinted his eyes as if trying to discern something obscure or mostly hidden. As he attempted to give the object back, Greapa gestured for him to show it to those nearby. Moshe happily rose and slowly walked around the inner circle of attendees, allowing them to examine the object. Others in rows further back were craning their necks to see what was in Moshe's hands. Some were standing on tiptoes. Those who could see the object clearly smiled in amazement, immediately recognizing the Hebrew that was written on it. Finally Greapa retrieved the object from Moshe and held it high for all to see.

In his hands Greapa held what looked like a piece of stone—marble, or perhaps granite—about twenty centimeters long by fifteen centimeters wide. On its front was a layer of gold attached to the stone. On the gold something was written. Greapa explained: "My father was a winemaker. Though we were not wealthy, we were somewhat well off. My Uncle Giovanni—my father's brother—was a printer by trade. He wanted to start his own business, but did not have the resources to do so. He came to my father asking for help. My father immediately gave him what he needed to start his business. A few years later he returned to my father to repay what my father had given him. He had been quite successful in his new business and out of gratitude he also gave my father this specially engraved plaque. It is a piece of granite with a thin golden plate attached. On that plate the Great Book is engraved in the languages with which it was originally written. The first line is written in letters that are about one centimeter tall. Each succeeding line is about nine tenths the height of the previous line. This continues until the letters are too small to make out with the naked eye. But with the lens you will see that the writing continues to get smaller and smaller until it becomes too small to make out even with the lens. If we had a lens strong enough we would see that the characters continue dwindling until they are somewhat more than a millionth of a meter in height. The writing then continues at that size for quite a while. Not only is the whole of the Great Book etched onto this tablet, but twenty-five copies of it are so inscribed. At the bottom right of the tablet you can see the mark of my uncle's business written in our ancient Italian language: *Stampa Eccellente di Giovanni.*

"My uncle's business was so adept that he could etch such microscopic writing into this gold. This was a testament to his achievement and prowess. My father treasured this little memento of his brother's success. I will leave it here overnight along with the lens for all to see and examine. Feel free to touch it and study it closely."

As people scanned the tablet they could read in Hebrew, which was the common language of the day, "In the beginning God created the heaven and the Earth, and the Earth became waste and empty, and darkness was upon the face of the abyss . . ." Their disappointment at having the speaking end just as the tale they were hearing was reaching a climax was swallowed by their amazement at the little plaque before them. Not one of them, save the five speakers, had ever seen anything so intricate and precise. They had no possible way to produce such an artifact. This was proof of an age that had a technology far different from theirs, a confirmation of the words that Greapa and the others had spoken.

As they proceeded home for the night, Greapa noticed something different. There was a lightness—a buoyancy—about and within them. Greama was beside him with her arm through his and her head resting on his shoulder. He thought he heard her cooing! All five of them were almost dancing their way back. Elizabeth broke into a laughing run and Benyamin, sporting a large grin, chased her. They were like young schoolmates, not thousand-year-olds. Even Moshe was chuckling. Something about the end of the meeting, something about that little golden plaque, had changed everything. The huge burden they had borne—in fact, *all* the people had borne—was lifted. Greapa did not understand it, but then again, he did not need to. The group was happy, even joyous. There was work yet to be done, but it seemed they had crested a peak and were now running downhill.

Addressing Moshe, Greapa asked, "Will you stay with us tonight?"

After considering for a moment he replied, "Yes, but only if I do not displace anyone."

Greapa stopped and gazed at Moshe, who also stopped and returned his gaze. Moshe's face was inscrutable. Greapa could detect nothing from his expression, but wondered, *Can he read my mind?* He and Greama had intended to give Moshe their room, while they would sleep in the small, but comfortable secondary guest quarters in the back of the house. Deciding to be bold, Greapa stretched forth his hand and placed it on Moshe's shoulder, then said, "As you wish." Moshe simply smiled warmly and gently patted his new friend's hand.

6

THE KING AND HIS KINGDOM

The five of them—those from the ancient age—sat at the table. The four younger ones had been invited elsewhere for an evening repast. As the ladies talked, Greapa noticed Moshe and Benyamin staring at him, quietly but pointedly. After a few minutes he finally asked, "What?"

Benyamin asked, "Are you going to finish the story?"

Moshe added, "Yes, how did you come by that plaque, given that nearly everything was destroyed in the upheavals?"

Greapa saw it was useless debating with these two eagle-eyed interrogators, and so began with a soft sigh. As he did, the ladies quieted to listen. "I mentioned earlier that my father was killed by the security forces of the ten-nation confederacy that became the Mediterranean empire ruled by the evil emperor. When my father died, his vineyard and belongings passed to my mother and me. I treasured that plaque and kept it in a hidden area beneath a slightly loose floorboard of our house. When the upheavals came I forgot about it completely. There were too many other matters of much greater importance to care for. When the final, great cataclysms struck the Mediterranean, my house with all the houses of our neighbors was leveled. The plaque never came to my mind after that, though if it had, I would have reckoned it destroyed or lost.

"As you know, eventually we were divided into groups and scattered across this continent. I was sent to this place, near where I had grown up. Not long after returning here—in fact, it was only a matter of a few days—the ruler of our new town, Lord Faithful, appeared to me. I had no idea what to expect from him and feared that some sort of discipline was about to be meted out to me, for at that time I did not really know what kind of person he was. Instead, he gently told me to follow him.

"He led me to the remains of a nearby town that had been completely demolished during the cataclysms. He walked me to a certain spot and told me the dig there. I knew that town, and even though it had become rubble I could still recognize what was there previously. It was the spot of a jeweler's shop. As I dug, I came across a few precious stones. I showed them to Lord Faithful, but he simply shook his head, so I threw them away. Finally I came across a fine brass loupe with a powerful lens. As I considered discarding it, Lord Faithful said, 'That!'

"I put it in my pocket as he led me to another spot, where a metalworker's gift shop once stood. Again he told me to dig. When I came across a beautiful and intact brass box with lid, he said again, 'That!'

"I held it in my hand as he led me elsewhere. It was quite a walk, but the day was beautiful: the air was clear, the sun shone, and it was balmy. So much had changed when the King returned. Although the surroundings had been greatly altered by those last years—roads barely walkable, greenery parched and burnt, dwellings demolished—as we walked, I knew where we were.

"When we arrived at what was once my home, I was flooded with memories of my father's murder, of my mother's death shortly before the end came, of friends and neighbors many of whom were no more, of the once stunning vineyard that had graced our land. Seeing the anguish on my face, Lord Faithful put his hand gently on my shoulder. The pain then subsided.

"He led me to the top of the debris that was once our dwelling. He pointed to a certain area and said, 'Dig there.' I slowly removed the stones and planks that covered the spot he had pointed to. Eventually I came to the undamaged floor of my own room. At once I recognized that loose floorboard where I had secreted the plaque. I looked up at Lord Faithful. He smiled and nodded. Underneath that floorboard the plaque lay without a scratch upon it! Lord Faithful said, 'Store the plaque and loupe in the box and seal it. Keep it safe. You may need them in the distant future.' I have kept it near me ever since, periodically checking and resealing the box as necessary. I never told anyone what its contents were, even Greama."

Greapa hesitated as if to stop the explanation there, but decided to continue. "Lord Faithful and I walked back together to this town, or rather what was at that time the beginning of this town. Although he was in some ways extraordinary, and different from us who were only human, we talked about human things, about the coming days, about the difficulties ahead, and mostly about the glorious future into which we were entering. As we walked I noticed that he was taking a somewhat circuitous route back, but I said nothing. We arrived about fifteen to twenty minutes later than we would have had we walked the same route as when we left, and we approached the area from a different direction.

"As we neared home—for that is what it was becoming—he smiled again and said, 'You will have a multitude of offspring, generation upon generation.' He then left—or, more accurately, disappeared. I watched, then turned to go to my lodging. As I did, Greama was walking by carrying something fairly heavy; as I recall it was a large, filled water bucket. Seeing the young—and very beautiful—woman in need, I asked her if I could help. She smiled gratefully and nodded.

"I handed her the brass box containing the plaque and loupe to hold, while I took the bucket from her hand. She never asked what was in the box. It seemed she was too occupied with our introduction and conversation.

"I was struck by her soft eyes, and as she introduced herself, by her gentle voice. We walked and talked, and the more she spoke, the more my heart was smitten. Remember, at that time we were all damaged within. We had been through things that were simply unbearable. Though we had survived by the divine hand of mercy, we were greatly traumatized. But this woman . . . ”—he choked a bit as he spoke—“this woman captured my heart. Somehow, in spite of my condition, my heart leapt within me as we walked together. I was only in my early twenties, but . . . ” Again he choked back the words. He looked to his wife of nearly a thousand years and simply cocked his head to one side, as he remembered the tenderness of that first encounter. Greama understood instantly and a tear ran down her cheek.

"That was how Carolyn and I met," Greapa managed.

Upon entering their room, Greapa and Greama found the smiling lord once again seated in the corner. He said, "Tomorrow is the *great* day!" and vanished, leaving the two of them shaking their heads in bewilderment. Looking at each other, they said in perfect unison, "What does he mean?" Laughing at themselves, they went to bed.

As the five of them seated themselves in the hall the next morning, the mood was uplifted, even joyful. The golden plaque and brass loupe lay on the small table in the hall's center. Based upon the innumerable fingerprints on it, the plaque must have been much handled the previous evening. Greapa mused, *Who would have thought a thousand years ago that such a small item as this plaque would one day have such a great impact?*

When all had quieted, Greapa rose, but rather than address the assembly as had been his norm, he turned and spoke to Moshe. "Would you honor us with a prayer to begin this meeting?"

Moshe stood immediately, closed his eyes, lifted his head to the heavens, and prayed aloud. "Dear Father—indeed, Father of all that is good and Source of all blessing—we bless *you* this morning! We bless and thank you for bringing us to this point. We praise you for what you are about to do as well. May every soul here and every one to whom this speaking travels take your words to heart, for your words bring salvation. We thank you for our King—your Firstborn, and we thank you for your many sons, who together lead us in your path of righteousness and life to you, yourself, the only true God. May your blessing be upon us today. Indeed, may you shower down blessing after blessing upon our open hearts! Hallelujah! We sing your Name, rejoice in your presence, and worship you for the marvels you have done, are doing, and will do. We praise you!"

Moshe then sat, at least temporarily, as Greapa set the stage for what was about to come: "As the many armies gathered to war in Israel—Russia from the north, the Asian horde from the east, and the emperor from the west and south—a series of divine judgments struck. It was as if the Earth and the whole universe was forcefully rejecting the emperor, his forces, his people, and all the other armies gathered to Israel. One grievous plague after another overtook the evil ones.

"Some kind of disease—a kind of microscopic germ—rose from the earth to infect the emperor's mark on all those who had received it. It was extremely virulent and painful. Then the Earth around and under the Mediterranean Sea erupted, spewing lava and huge amounts of slag and mud. This turned the sea into a kind of thick, blood-red sludge, like the blood of a dead man, and the rivers into a blood-red, undrinkable, thick fluid of some sort. The sun itself then erupted, spewing out huge flares of intensely hot plasma. These scorched all who were exposed to the sun. Yet, rather than repent to the God who had power over these plagues, they blasphemed him.

"Next, the greatest of all darknesses fell upon Rome—the emperor's capital—and the whole of the emperor's kingdom. This darkness caused a huge drain on all the power reserves used to produce electricity. As the power supply dwindled, the great device—the ultrafast computer—that controlled all those with the emperor's mark recognized that what it needed to maintain its functionality and control was rapidly waning. In an effort to force men to supply it with more power, it caused excruciating pain in all those with the mark. Men gnawed their tongues for the pain. They screamed in agony and rolled on the ground from the torment. Yet, still they blasphemed God rather than repent.

"A great earthquake then shook the whole of the emperor's kingdom and the Middle East. Rome began burning and there was no stopping the flames. The great river Euphrates dried up, the sources of its water having been diverted elsewhere by the earthquake. This allowed the great Asian hordes, which had by that time joined forces, to cross the Euphrates and advance toward Israel."

As Greapa described each of these plagues, a brief vision played before his listeners, who winced at each one as if being stung by mild electric shocks.

Greama stood to relate the happenings where she was at that time. "In the United States all the Christians suddenly changed in appearance and were caught up into the clouds. I saw this with my own eyes. I recall wondering fearfully, *If God is taking the Christians from the Earth, what will become of us and this whole planet?*"

Moshe began a long description of the decisive events in Israel. "Many of us were still in Jerusalem—we knew many secret places to hide from the emperor's vicious forces. We moved from one space to another constantly to avoid detection and slaughter.

"The clouds overhead were incredibly dense. Neither the sun nor the moon could be seen. The darkness covering the Earth was intense and thick, almost tangible. We were at an end—without hope, without a future, without strength, in utter despair. There was nothing left to us. Israel was nearly totally destroyed. About two-thirds of its people had died already. Much of Jerusalem had been reduced to rubble. What we saw as our last chance of salvation—the two ancient witnesses—lay dead before us in the street. We saw only our deaths before us and the obliteration of our beloved country. But then it seemed as if time itself stopped: the emperor's armies began to prepare for the battle with the other forces entering Israel, and the great tribulation we had endured ended abruptly.

"To the astonishment of us all, Moses and Elijah, who had been dead for three and a half days, suddenly stood on their feet. The emperor's forces and their sympathizers shook with fear when this happened. A great voice rang out, 'Come up here!' and the two ancient ones disappeared into the heavens in a cloud. Then the Earth started to tremble as another great earthquake shook us. About a tenth of the city was destroyed in that tremor and many thousands of the renowned among the emperor's followers were killed. While they were terrified, we gave glory to God. The slightest glimmer of hope had sprung up within us.

"The stars began to fall from the heavens. To our shock and great amazement a sign—as it were, a burning cross—appeared in the clouds above us." Again the visions began before the audience, first of the darkness, then of the falling stars, and then of the great, heavenly sign.

Moshe continued: "As quickly as the sign appeared, it vanished, leaving us again in darkness—a darkness unimaginably thick, for it was a darkness that was upon our own hearts. As the light began to dawn within us and we saw what we had done in rejecting Jesus and how we had been fighting against him those many centuries—denying who he was and what he had done, we wept, we mourned, we cried out for forgiveness. The whole of Israel—every soul remaining—cried out with tears, "Jesus, save us! Lord Jesus, save us!"

The whole of the hall was enveloped in the deepest of blacknesses, as those there tasted of that great moment in the history of Israel. Greapa quickly looked about and saw the entranced audience on chair's edge.

"And then," Moshe continued, "and then the heavens parted ..." The dark vision before them cracked open, and the blazing, blinding figure of the glorious Christ appeared. Many of the transfixed listeners tried to shield their eyes from the brightness of His appearing, but to no avail. The glory shined through to every heart. And he was not alone. Following him were many thousands—no, many millions—of angels and of those of his followers who had matured in his divine life. If the audience were not so gripped by what they were seeing, Greapa was sure they would have broken into cheers and applause at Christ's coming to save Israel and the whole Earth.

Though overwhelmed by what he was seeing for the second time, Moshe managed to speak on. "We never, *never* imagined what we were seeing would occur. The Lord Christ was coming to save Israel with the millions of his heavenly armies. They swarmed through the air, circling like an enormous flock of vultures over the doomed forces that had invaded us," he said, as the vision of the heavenly armies filled the hall.

"He first fought at Bozrah, to the south and east of Jerusalem. He fought not with fists or physical might of any kind. He fought simply with his almighty word. He spoke and it came to pass. As he worked his way north, enemy after enemy died at his word.

"He struck the horses of the armies with madness and their riders as well. The forces began to fight with each other, imagining that their own companions were their greatest danger. How many were killed in this fashion, I do not know. Others fired weapons at the King and his armies. Not only did these do no harm to the heavenly spiritual forces, but they succeeded in killing many of their own soldiers. Still others were struck with a plague from the brightness of the Lord's appearing. Their flesh melted from their skeletons. As the slaughter of the millions of invaders continued, blood rose in the lowland valley that runs north to south up to the bridles of the horses.

"He finally came to Jerusalem, where we were in grave danger from the forces still there. As he descended to the Mount of Olives, the greatest of all earthquakes convulsed the Earth." The vision of the Lord Christ descending appeared. All in the hall sat agape and mesmerized. "We felt Jerusalem being lifted up violently by the shuddering Earth. Great rocks were hurled into the sky, and then fell upon the opposing armies. They blasphemed God rather than repent. As the Lord's feet touched the Mount of Olives, it split in two from east to west. We heard a voice commanding us to flee, which we all—every one of us—did. We fled into that valley in the cleft of the Mount of Olives. And in the shadow of that valley we perceived the unbearable brightness of the Lord's appearing pass over us and vaporize many of the opposers. We then heard yet another command, 'Fight! *Fight!*' The Spirit of our God was upon us. We came forth with vengeance to take back what God had given to us. Every one of us fought against the remnant of the invaders. The weakest among us fought like King David, and the strong fought like God. We used whatever was at hand as weapons, and as the enemies fell before us, we took their weapons, and used them to slaughter more of those same enemies.

"From there, the Lord Jesus moved north to Har-Magedon. This was the last stand for all those challenging God. The Russian armies fell upon the mountains of northern Israel as they stormed southward. The Asian horde was slaughtered from the eastern border of Israel westward. There at Har-Magedon the emperor with his cohort, the prime minister, and their army, fought to the last man against the King. Every single one of them died save for those two beasts—for that is what they were—the emperor and the prime minister. They were taken alive and brought before the Lord. Fire from the mouth of the Lord swept them alive into the lake that burns with fire, which is with us to this day as you all have seen. Then it was over.

"Birds—hawks, eagles, vultures, and even those that by nature are not birds of prey—flocked by the millions, or perhaps billions, throughout Israel to feast upon the flesh of those the King had destroyed. Every one of his enemies became a meal for the hungry fowl."

The whole hall was filled with exhausted yet exuberant listeners. Greapa smiled and spoke, "Let us take a few minutes to breathe and regain our strength. Dear Moshe's narrative has been quite consuming!"

Greapa retrieved some fruit for the four of them from Greama. As he took a bite, he thought, *Sweet and juicy! Just like I most enjoy.* They sat and watched the reactions of those about them. Eyes still wide and excited chatter abounded.

They still had more to share for this morning's meeting, so Greapa stood and started to calm the somewhat boisterous crowd.

"Let us take our seats. There is yet more to say." He paused, then spoke: "When the King appeared, we all saw him. Though we were hundreds or even thousands of kilometers away, we saw him. Even Greama, who was on the other side of the globe, saw him." Greama nodded her head vigorously.

Greapa continued, "And when that last, great earthquake struck Jerusalem, it affected the whole Earth. Across the globe, and particularly on this continent, all the cities that remained standing after the previous calamities fell. The emperor's capital—Rome—fell into the sea, never to be seen again. Islands disappeared; mountains were leveled. It was that great! It was astounding that any of us survived.

"Then suddenly, all the upheaval and violence completely stopped, and calm reigned. The Lord—the invincible King—had destroyed all his enemies! It was surreal. Satan—the source of all the problems on Earth—was then bound and his deception of the people ended for a thousand years.

"The King sent forth his angels to gather out of his kingdom everything offensive, to gather the elect of the Jews—those chosen by God to enter the kingdom—who had been scattered by the prime minister and emperor during those last years of tumult, and to gather all the peoples remaining on Earth, both good and bad, to Israel. Many of us brought with us the Jews we had cared for, carrying them on horses or carts. The angels led us, and were quite determined that none would stay behind. Every living soul was brought to Israel.

"It took us a number of days to reach the Holy Land, and would have taken far longer except for the angelic aid we were afforded. We arrived shortly before the Jewish feast of Yom Kippur. The Jews were taken to Jerusalem to stand before the King. We of the nations were settled in the valley of Jehoshaphat to await the King. The angels ministered to our needs during those days."

Moshe then spoke of the happenings in Jerusalem. "Once the King appeared in the sky above Israel, the end came startlingly quickly. The invading forces were completely eliminated and those two beastly and vile persons—the emperor and the prime minister—were cast alive into that burning lake. Only we, and Christ with his armies, were left in the Holy Land. The King immediately sent out his angels to gather all the Jews that had been scattered throughout the Earth. During that time, we did our best to tend to those of us who had been injured—and there were many. Over the next few days our fellow Israelis arrived in small groups from wherever they had been sent as captives. It took about a week for all who had been dispersed to be returned. Immediately prior to Yom Kippur—our Day of Atonement—the King addressed us face-to-face.

"It is very difficult to convey what happened during that encounter. The Lord Jesus spoke calmly and gently, but each and every word was like a knife slicing into and through our hearts. The light within us—the brilliant rays of a spiritual sunrise—was nearly unbearable. What we were, how we were, what we had done, what our nation had done was fully and completely revealed. In the great mercy of God, our hearts had been softened to receive the truth and repent. He spoke of how he had repeatedly stretched out his hand to us in love over the centuries, only to be repeatedly rejected. He then showed us his hands marked with the imprints of the nails of his crucifixion and the wound in his side from the spear of that Roman soldier; and then we saw him hanging on the cross. That broke the heart of every one of us. We wept and wailed. That Day of Atonement was for the very first time real. We all mourned that day—each family apart, the fathers and children apart, and the wives apart by themselves. We mourned that day and for days more. The Spirit of God was upon us, convicting us of our great sins and also forgiving us. We emerged from this depth of sorrow a different people: humbled, lowly, realizing our great lack of God. Then we accompanied the King and his believers to witness his judgment upon the nations.

"We then enjoyed a real Feast of Tabernacles—Sukkot. For the first time in the history of Israel we enjoyed a true peace, as the King of Peace reigned in Jerusalem. We then began the daunting task of restoring the Temple, Jerusalem, and the entirety of Israel.

"We first removed everything offensive from the Temple and the Temple Mount, starting with that vile image of the emperor. Once its power reserves had been depleted during the great darkness that covered the Earth, it had become nothing more than a motionless hulk. We threw it into the burning lake where the emperor—the one who was imaged—had found his eternal destiny. In fact, we threw everything offensive into that fire.

"It took us a couple of weeks to restore the Temple and once again offer sacrifices, this time remembering the great sacrifice of himself that Christ had offered for us. It then took about another month and a half to establish the priesthood in Jerusalem. It was a full seven years before the land of Israel was finally and fully cleansed of the great armies who had overrun us. Over those seven years their bones were found repeatedly throughout the country and disposed of."

Having finished his speaking, Moshe sat. Greapa then told of the fate of the nations. "As I mentioned previously, when we arrived in Israel we were taken to the valley of Jehoshaphat. There were surprisingly few of us gathered there, perhaps a few tens of millions. As I look back on those days now, with the knowledge of the events of that time I now possess, I am no longer surprised. The Earth's population had numbered in the billions. But consider how many had died: many died when those first asteroids shook the earth; when the initial onslaught of the great asteroid swarm struck and the great burning mountain struck the Pacific, perhaps a billion or more died in Asia alone and hundreds of millions more died along the rim of the Pacific; untold millions died elsewhere during those upheavals; then the great Asian horde—which in itself numbered a couple hundred million—rampaged across Asia, killing about another third of mankind; and finally, many died in Israel at the Lord's return. In addition, all of the Christians had been removed from the Earth. As a consequence, only relatively few of the nations remained.

"We awaited the King with trepidation. Many among us had harmed the Jews or the Christians. We had no idea what our fate would be. The day came, and we stood before the King as he sat on his throne of glory. He commanded his angels, and they separated us into two groups, one on his right hand, the other on his left. The four of us—Benyamin, Elizabeth, Greama, and I—were on his right. He addressed our group first: 'Come, blessed of my Father, inherit the kingdom prepared for you from the foundation of the world: for I was hungry, and you gave me to eat; I was thirsty, and you gave me drink; I was a stranger, and you took me in; naked, and you clothed me; I was sick, and you visited me; I was in prison, and you came unto me.' I cannot tell you of the relief, the joy, the peace I felt—we in that group *all* felt—at his words. But we did not understand them. We asked when we had done such things. He said, 'Truly I say to you, when you did it to one of the least of these my brothers, you did it to me.' There was a pleased joy in his voice as he spoke to us—a joy that lingers with us to this day." Greapa looked to his two friends and to Greama, and even then could see the eternal relief in their faces.

"He then turned to those on his left and told them to depart from him into the eternal fire prepared for the devil and his angels, for they had not helped his brothers when they were in need. Indeed, many among them had harmed the Lord's brothers in one way or another. Jesus spoke with a profound, heart-wrenching sadness. He did not want to condemn, but these cursed ones had chosen the path into destruction in spite of the angelic warning they had received. They were removed from us and thrown into that same fire where the emperor and the prime minister had been cast. God's judgment was finished; a new age had begun. We were the seeds of humanity that was to again fill the Earth.

"The angels then separated us into small groups of one or two hundred. There seemed to be no pattern or logic to the groupings. Greama, Benyamin, Elizabeth, and I were all in the same cluster of people. However, none of us knew any of the others in our group. We were then led to this very area on which we now meet. It was devoid of any kind of structure. In fact, virtually every building on Earth had been reduced to rubble by the great cataclysms of the end. None of us had anything to which we could return! We all were starting a new life together.

"As we talked among ourselves as to how we should begin the formidable task of this new existence, Lord Faithful appeared to us. At first, he said nothing. Rather, he walked through our midst looking deeply at each of us. Many of us were suffering from wounds received from the great earthquake and the other judgments that had struck the Earth—some of the wounds serious. I myself had a badly broken arm, which I held close to my chest with a sling. It was quite painful. He healed each and every one of us by a touch or a word. There was a gentleness and a peace about him that was like a balm to the wounds of our hearts. We had experienced incredible and unspeakable things; we were exhausted in every way. But his presence and touch were mercifully uplifting.

"It was quite clear that Lord Faithful was to rule over us—his manner, his shining countenance, and his authority all spoke this. But he did not say he was to be our lord or king, although we knew he was. He simply said that he would be taking care of us. He said that the ground on which we stood was to become our home. He told us our highest priorities would be shelter, food, and water, although we lacked even rudimentary tools with which to begin. But he then led us to a nearby underground storage area that had many of the necessities we would need. It must have been stocked by a thoughtful person in previous years, but for whatever reason, never used. There we found food and tools of various sorts.

"The lord then broke us into smaller groups to which he assigned certain tasks: one group to make temporary shelters, another to handle food production and preparation, a third to provide water, and so forth. I was in the food production company. Given my background on my father's vineyard, I knew much about plants, plantings, fertilization, and harvesting, so it seemed more than fortuitous that I was assigned to that group. In fact, all of us in that company had some background in agriculture. It was there that Benyamin and I first met. After a few days together, I started calling him the Apricot Man and he named me Mr. Vineyard! We became very close friends.

"There were much-needed miracles in those days. The Earth was a shambles—the waters were damaged, much of the flora was burned or destroyed, and roads were nearly impassable. The lord healed the river that passes through our town with a single word! That water was still blood-red and undrinkable. He walked up to it and simply said, 'Heal.' The water started to clear in front of our eyes, and then became like flowing crystal before us and stretching out in both directions. He turned to us and said with a warm smile, 'Taste and see.' That water was indescribably delicious!

"Those first days and months were hard—indeed, very hard. But there was something different, something in the atmosphere, something in everything we did, or touched, or consumed. It made us beside ourselves with joy and peace. We were full of energy and hope! What is more, everything we did was blessed. The ground bore foods of all kinds in amazing abundance; the climate cooperated to water our plants, but not overwater; the differences of our past lives were swallowed in the blessings of that new age. Even the differences in our languages disappeared—we all spontaneously spoke the same tongue that we all to this day still speak.

"After a few months, Lord Faithful spoke to us all, telling us we would be going up to Jerusalem on the Passover to celebrate the feast there, and to present ourselves before the King. We would go up every year to observe the Passover. I can recall that first Passover vividly. We came to Jerusalem and ascended to the peak with unspeakable joy and singing. I do not know how we all—every one of us who had been blessed at the King's right hand—could fit, but we did. We saw the King again! Oh, how blessed we were! He was smiling as he surveyed us all, and his words to us were so deeply moving. He told us to replenish the Earth with the joy and love of God, his Father, blessing our every moment. There was and is something about him that is so attractive that to this day we yearn yet more and more to be like he is.

"We returned to our village—it was still quite small—and it was not long before the first children were born into our blessed age. There were children, upon children, upon children! There were countless children who then bore a third generation of offspring. This replenishing of the Earth has gone on for nearly a thousand years up to this very day. And so we have come full circle.

Greapa paused for some time. He surveyed the audience and considered. He chose his next words carefully. "This brings us to the point of all this speaking—something crucial, vital, and critical. We have spoken with great purpose of the things past, and particularly of the darkness of the previous age and of God's judgments upon that evil. That darkness—that evil—is coming again," Greapa announced with utmost gravity and sincerity. He turned about, gazing at each person before him and repeated, *"That darkness—that evil—is coming again."* The gathering was stunned by this sudden change in his speaking. He repeated yet a third time, and loudly, *"That darkness—that evil—is coming again!"* Questioning whispers broke out between the attendees: "When? How? What is he saying?"

Greapa garnered all his strength as he thought, *This must penetrate.* "It is true that Satan was bound, as I told you. But he was only *temporarily* bound. He will be released from his chain in about twenty years. He will come forth with all his great subtlety, using subterfuge and deception to try to mislead all the peoples on Earth into attempting to destroy the King and his brothers. Those of us who passed through that dark time know him and his machinations. He will not deceive us. *But you . . . you* have never experienced him, his darkness, his evil, his supremely subtle means of manipulation. He will hide himself. He will try to make you think that the evil things you imagine are from your own minds. He will pretend to be you within you. He will try to twist your hearts. He will tell you dark lies. He will say that the previous age was good and that the King is evil because he destroyed it. He will tempt you to say evil, to do evil, to practice evil until you and the evil become one. He will do all this without acknowledging that these evil things come from him, the great and hidden fallen angel. This is how he will try to destroy mankind. *Do not listen to him!*

"He will tempt you to think that what he proffers is pleasurable, but will hide from you that in practicing these evils you will destroy your own souls. If you listen to him, he will guide your minds and hearts into the depths of his darkness, and from there he will persuade you to attack the King and the King's brothers.

He will tell you how wonderful the previous age was, how great the many devices were of which he, himself, was the originator. He will tell you that in the previous age those devices enabled men to travel faster, entertain themselves more, and greatly limit the amount of work they had to do, but he will not tell you that those devices, when used, work subtly in men's souls to defile, corrupt, and destroy. *Do not listen to him!*

"We have told you of this beforehand so that when this darkness comes you will have a witness of truth to help guard you and lead you through that time of trial to the eternal blessing that awaits those who overcome that evil. We will be here, but how many will believe the lies that will be said about us? Take all our words to heart, that when that day comes you will overcome." With that, Greapa nodded to Joseph and sat.

Joseph stood and, with a word of thanks to God, dismissed the meeting. Though still amazed at what they had just heard, many of the onlookers came forward to thank Greapa, Greama, Benyamin, and Elizabeth, and to particularly meet and thank Moshe.

It was some time before the five of them managed to leave the hall and start their way home. Before going, Greapa carefully stowed the golden plaque with the loupe back into the brass box. It was a memory of his cherished father.

They walked at a leisurely pace, with the sense that their responsibility was finished, at least this part of it. Moshe then said, "It is time for me to return to the King. His servant waits for me. I have learned much here. We do not often have the opportunity to spend time with those who are not Jews. I have come to appreciate you in a much deeper way." He blessed them, giving each the godly farewell of the priests. As he walked off toward the town's edge, he hesitated, then turned back and spoke, "My friends, when you next come to Jerusalem, ask for Simon, the keeper of the priests' quarters. He will know where I am." He smiled, nodded, and walked out of sight.

As the remaining four of them continued their way home, talking one to another, a fifth joined them from the side. At first, they did not notice his company. Eventually, Greapa started at the presence of the newcomer. Looking at him closely, Greapa did not recognize him, nor did the other three. "Hello, Sir, can we help you?" queried Greapa as he thought, *There is something about this newcomer that is vaguely familiar—something about his mannerisms, or perhaps it is his bearing. Yes! His bearing!* But before Greapa could utter the proper greeting, Lord Faithful smiled broadly and said, "Well done! Very well done indeed!" and vanished in the divine brilliance.

EPILOGUE

Greapa and Greama relaxed at the dining room table. The recent days had been demanding, but their task was finished, at least for the moment. Later would come the gathering of all the transcriptions, the editing, and the eventual book production. While they did not have the technologies of those old and evil times, they did have the means needed for their task. It took them more time, but in this wonderful age, their days were slow and easy. There were no more devilish taskmasters.

With them were Joshua, Sarah, Benyamin, Elizabeth, Nathanael, and Mira. The latter couples were ready to leave on their journeys home. The table showed signs of mostly consumed morning victuals. "Delicious as usual," mused Greapa, who received a nod of agreement from Greama and the others.

Nathanael gazed intently and inquiringly at Greapa, who looked back with the unspoken answer, "What is it you want to know?" Nathanael asked, "How did you get the name Greapa? It is certainly not a common name. In fact, I have never heard of anyone else called by it. Was it given to you at birth?"

Greapa looked at Greama, who gave him the slightest of shrugs, as if to say *Why not?* So Greapa proceeded. "It has been a very long time since anyone even asked that question, Nathanael.

It seems everyone simply takes our names for granted. But therein lies a brief, but amusing tale.

After we were first married some 979 years ago, we of course had children, who called us Father and Mother, or more affectionately Papa and Mama. Then *they* had children, to whom we became Grandpa and Grandma. Then, when those children in turn had children, we became Great Grandpa and Great Grandma. At some point our names became too long. So, by agreement we became known as Great Pa and Great Ma.

One day one of the little toddlers—Lisa by name—came running into our living room, where I was reading. She was learning to speak and could not quite pronounce all of her words yet. When she attempted to call my name—Great Pa—she twisted the words somewhat and out came Greapa! The name was spoken with such affection from the little one that it immediately brought a great smile to my face. Seeing my delight at her slip of the tongue, she then started shouting the name, "Greapa! Greapa! Greapa!"

Greama, who was in the kitchen, heard the shouts and came quickly in to see what all the commotion was. Little Lisa was still shouting, "Greapa!" Seeing the tickled look on my face and then the astonishment on Greama's face as she entered, Lisa stopped, thought for a second, and then started shouting, "Greama! Greama! Greama!" Well, we so loved both the names and their origin that we have kept them to this day. It is our loving testimony to dear Lisa. This happened so long ago that all those who were there at the time have passed, so the source of our names has remained hidden for many years.

Heart-touched by such a sweet story, Nathanael nodded a half smile. But there was still a question in his eyes. Greapa cocked his head as if to ask, "What?" So Nathanael inquired, "But then what is your birth name?" The ancient man glowed as he smiled mirthfully at Greama, Benyamin, and Elizabeth, turned back to Nathanael and said, "Just call me Greapa."

www.ingramcontent.com/pod-product-compliance
Lightning Source LLC
Chambersburg PA
CBHW072008170626
46813CB00005B/2071